F
Dudley, Ernest.
Dr Morelle intervenes

DR. MORELLE INTERVENES

Doctor Morelle and Miss Frayle await the last train to London ... at its approach, the village station attendant rushes to open the level crossing gates. Later, however, on the train, they learn that following a fatal crash, the station's level crossing had been replaced by a bridge! Exactly five years earlier the stationmaster had been killed as he vainly attempted to open the gates. And on the anniversary of the disaster, it's reputed that his ghost returns ...

ERNEST DUDLEY

DR. MORELLE INTERVENES

Complete and Unabridged

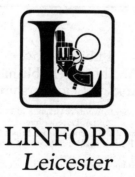

LINFORD
Leicester

First published in Great Britain

First Linford Edition
published 2010

British Library CIP Data

Dudley, Ernest.
    Dr Morelle intervenes. - -
    (Linford mystery library)
    1. Morelle, Doctor (Fictitious character)- -
    Fiction. 2. Detective and mystery stories.
    3. Large type books.
    I. Title II. Series
    823.9'14–dc22

    ISBN 978–1–44480–342–6

Published by
F. A. Thorpe (Publishing)
Anstey, Leicestershire

Set by Words & Graphics Ltd.
Anstey, Leicestershire
Printed and bound in Great Britain by
T. J. International Ltd., Padstow, Cornwall

This book is printed on acid-free paper

1

The case of the Telbury Halt Ghost

Doctor Morelle was the type of person who was at all times very content with his own company. He was, nevertheless, on terms of acquaintance with rather more people than the average person, most of them being with men with whom he shared a common interest in the field of science or medicine, or with a somewhat more varied group — those individuals with whom he had come into contact upon his numerous investigations of a criminological nature.

While he would hardly be described as 'rubbing shoulders with members of the underworld as well as members of the police forces in various parts of the globe' — the Doctor would have resented the description in any case for its inelegance of phrase! — he had, however, a mixed circle of acquaintances.

He received numerous invitations from these persons who were anxious — as he was quick to appreciate! — to improve the acquaintance. But he rarely accepted any of them. On the other hand, there was one he never refused if he found it possible to spare the time, and that was an invitation from old Professor Cosmo Wade. Wade lived in a delightful Georgian mansion at Telbury, a tiny village near Oxford. He telephoned one evening asking if the Doctor could come down that weekend. He had, he explained, with some excitement, just completed some interesting experiments with certain fauna obtained from the shores of the Aegean, and he was anxious for Doctor Morelle's opinion concerning them. And so, accompanied by Miss Frayle (she would be most useful in collating any notes on the Professor's work, for he was well aware that the old man failed utterly in regard to any methodical system of filing or tabulation) Doctor Morelle drove down late on Saturday to Telbury.

It had proved a pleasant weekend, the results of the Professor's research had absorbed the Doctor. True, from Miss Frayle's point of view it had hardly been a satisfactory holiday. The weather had been bitterly cold; snow had fallen soon after they had arrived, and it was still snowing on Sunday night as they prepared to return to London.

'Are you sure you won't stay until the morning?' Wade tried to persuade the Doctor as they stood in the hall saying their 'goodbyes'.

Doctor Morelle shook his head.

'You are most hospitable,' he said, 'but I have an important appointment at an early hour in the morning.' And, pulling on his gloves, he urged Miss Frayle out of the front door away from the hospitable warmth and into night and the snowstorm that had now reached a considerable pitch. 'Come, Miss Frayle, let us confront the elements, and refrain from shivering in that ridiculous fashion. You cannot possibly feel chilled in your thick wrappings!'

In a few moments they were in his car, nosing cautiously along the narrow country lanes, which were treacherously deep in snow. They succeeded in making good progress, however, for the first few miles, and Doctor Morelle was enlarging upon his abilities as a motorist, no matter what the circumstances or conditions, when one of the cylinders began to miss. Finally the engine gave out altogether, barely giving him time to pull the car into one side of the road. He quickly switched on his dashboard light and rapidly checked the dials. They seemed to be in order. He pressed the self-starter button. There was no response from the engine.

'Oh dear!' said Miss Frayle apprehensively. 'I wonder what can be wrong?'

'I fear the worst!' he snapped irritably.

She glanced at his face, shadowed and more saturnine than ever in the glow of the dashboard light. His lips were drawn in a thin bitter line.

'Can't you do anything, Doctor? You don't mean we're caught in this terrible blizzard?' And she shuddered at the idea.

He made no reply. After a moment he lit a cigarette.

'I think I may reassure you on that point,' he murmured. 'We would appear to have reached the main road. Doubtless a vehicle of some nature will shortly overtake us and we can obtain assistance.'

It seemed, however, that this optimism was not to be realised. Very few cars appeared to be venturing out that night. For what Miss Frayle thought must be hours they sat listening to the wind whistling in the trees overhead, and watched the snow pile up steadily against the windscreen. Suddenly, during a temporary abatement of the wind, they heard the sound of an approaching car. In a few moments it drew alongside, and its driver and Doctor Morelle lowered their side-windows simultaneously. The shadowy figure of a man was at the wheel of the other car.

'Am I right for Telbury Halt?' His voice had a harsh quality, and Miss Frayle imagined that his face was white, in the dim light and bore a strained, almost anxious expression.

'I fear,' Doctor Morelle began, 'I have no idea as to the whereabouts of a railway station. Perhaps you could, however, assist me — ?'

But the man had let in his clutch and the car was driving quickly away. Miss Frayle clutched the Doctor's arm.

'Doctor!' she gasped. 'Did — did you notice there was someone in the back seat? All muffled up so that you couldn't see who it was — ?'

He laughed shortly.

'My dear Miss Frayle, your somewhat over-fertile imagination is apt to run away with you!'

'Well, he's run away from *us*!' was her quick reply.

His eyes glittered in the shadows of his face. There may have been a quirk of amusement at the corners of his mouth. She went on nervously:

'That shows there was something wrong! Or why did they drive off like that without waiting to answer you?'

'It certainly betrayed a lack of courtesy on his part,' he conceded. 'But if one suspected everyone of criminal intent merely because of their ill manners, one would be able to point to very few as being innocent!'

'Well, I've a feeling — ' she was about

to persist, when he interrupted her with a sardonic chuckle:

'That feminine intuition of yours!' he mocked.

Miss Frayle gave him a hurt look from behind her spectacles and said no more. They sat silently for a few minutes. Then he began to pull his coat collar up round his ears.

'What are you going to do?' she asked.

'From what I remember of this stretch of road, we should be within walking distance of a village.'

'You're going to walk in this?' she indicated the falling snow.

'That is my intention. Unless you imagine I can conjure up a team of reindeer and a sleigh out of the storm and drive off in the manner of Santa Claus!'

Anyone less like that benign old gentleman she couldn't imagine! She was about to make some remark to the effect that he would look very funny as Father Christmas when she decided he might take her seriously, and refrained. She said instead:

'I'll come too. I can't stay here alone.'

'My dear Miss Frayle, your footwear is quite inadequate to withstand these conditions. You would merely catch a severe cold, which would cause me considerable inconvenience. We have a busy week ahead of us. You will be perfectly safe here, I can reassure you. Lock all the doors if that affords you any satisfaction.'

And, in spite of her protests at being left alone, he got out, slammed the door, and disappeared into the swirling snow-flakes. She took him at his word, secured the doors and huddled in her coat, trembling with apprehension, expecting any moment that horrible menacing figures would loom up out of the storm.

It seemed hours, but actually it was only twenty minutes by the clock on the dashboard when she saw an ancient car with rather uncertain headlights come chugging along towards her. She gazed at it with a fast-beating heart as a heavily muffled little man sprang out, then her trepidation subsided when she saw the Doctor's tall gaunt shape follow him. The man lost no time in removing the bonnet of Doctor Morelle's car, making a hasty inspection with the help of a large torch. He swung the starting handle once or twice, listened, and shook his head dubiously. He grunted:

'Take more'n five minutes to fix that, I reckon!'

'You mean you can't do it tonight?' Doctor Morelle frowned.

'Not a chance!' he said with finality. 'Take the best part of a working day.' And he went off into a string of technical terms in explanation of what was amiss. The Doctor's face wore a bitter look.

'This is very unfortunate. I particularly wish to return to London tonight.'

The little man scratched his head. Then he suggested:

'Tell you what, I'll tow your car in to my garage. Then I'll run you on to Telbury Halt in my old 'bus. It's only a mile further on the station is.' He glanced at his watch. 'You'll just about catch the ten-twenty to London — last train up!'

Doctor Morelle had no alternative but to fall in with his suggestion, which he did somewhat ungraciously. At last he and

Miss Frayle had been towed with considerable difficulty through the snow into the village, safely garaged, and they set off for Telbury Halt in the little man's car. The snow had abated somewhat, but the wind blew as furiously as ever as they drove up the incline to a bleak little railway station its entrance illuminated by two oil lamps, flickering uncertainly, which swung creakingly with every howling gust.

Miss Frayle hurried into the station while the Doctor made arrangements with the garage man concerning his car, and remunerated him for his trouble. As she passed under the corrugated roof over the station entrance she noticed a set of tyre marks in the snow indicating, apparently, that a car had pulled up and driven on again. It occurred to her casually that it might be the car with the mysterious driver which had passed them. This in turn suggested that one of the occupants might be inside the station. Which one? she wondered with mounting curiosity. She paused at the door and waited for Doctor Morelle to join her.

She said nothing to him as they went in together, and the tyre-tracks seemed to have passed unnoticed by him.

The waiting room, however, was empty. While she remained behind, the Doctor went out onto the platform. He returned after a few moments declaring he had walked the length of the platform and pronounced it deserted and the parcels-office locked.

'We would appear to be the only passengers,' he said.

'You don't think the train's gone?'

He glanced at his watch. 'Not unless it made its departure fifteen minutes before the time scheduled.'

Miss Frayle wondered what had happened to the people in the car. Perhaps they didn't want to catch the train at all, she decided. Just wanted to make some inquiries and then continue their journey.

'Still permitting that imagination of yours to run riot!' murmured Doctor Morelle, without glancing up from a slim book he had produced and was reading. It was a scientific treatise the Professor had lent him. Miss Frayle gave him a startled look. His uncanny gift for apparently divining her thoughts continued to astonish her, while at the same time it discomfited her. It wasn't natural for anyone to be able to see right into your mind like that! The Doctor chuckled sardonically at her expression and went on reading. She was silent and crossed to the fireplace. The fire, however, was almost out. The hearth was piled with ashes, which did not appear to have been removed for several days. She shivered, drew her coat closer, and gazed round the little, dimly-lit waiting room. It appeared to serve as a booking-hall also. She noticed that the door next to the ticket-window was ajar. Summoning her courage, she went over to it and cautiously put her head round the door. She was greeted with an agreeable waft of warm air from a large oil stove. The office was empty. An incandescent oil lamp glimmered somewhat fitfully, though it gave more illumination than the one in the waiting room, and the place seemed comparatively cheerful.

'There's a much better light in here,

Doctor Morelle — it's warm too,' she called to him. He looked up from his book.

'Are you also implying that it is unoccupied?'

'There's no one here.'

He appeared suitably impressed by the prospect of some warmth and better light and, joining her, preceded her into the office.

'I think, under the circumstances, we might presume to trespass upon the railway's hospitality!' he murmured, promptly appropriating the only chair, a large office chair under the light. Miss Frayle dragged up a stool upon which she perched, and spread her hands before the warmth from the stove. In the confined space the only sound was the sputter of the lamp and the stove and the rustle of the Doctor's book. Outside the wind howled around the little station.

'I wonder what can have become of the booking-clerk?' presently speculated Miss Frayle.

The Doctor turned a page and blew out a cloud of cigarette smoke. 'No doubt

occupied in one of his other capacities
— porter, stationmaster or signalman, or
whatever offices he combines with that of
booking-office attendant.'

She nodded drowsily. The warmth
from the stove was inclined to send her
into a doze. She didn't hear the door
open a few minutes later, though
Doctor Morelle had caught the sound
of soft footsteps outside, and a pair of
feet and trousers moved into his line of
vision. He looked up from his book to
see a middle-aged man, greying slightly
at the temples, standing in the doorway
staring at them. He wore an official
looking cap that was rather soiled, and
carried a small suitcase. 'Evenin',' he
muttered, and Miss Frayle woke up
with a start and nearly fell off her
perch.

'Good evening,' murmured the Doctor,
eyeing the newcomer speculatively.

The man half closed the door and
placed the suitcase beside it. Then he
crossed over to the ticket-window and
pushed up the flap with a sharp bang.

From his action Miss Frayle, gathering

her sleep-fuddled wits about her, concluded with a twinge of embarrassment
that it was in the nature of a hint that
she and the Doctor were on the wrong
side of the ticket-window. She glanced at
Doctor Morelle who seemed, however, to
have become absorbed in his book once
more.

She explained to the man nervously:

'I — I hope you don't mind us
warming ourselves here? But it was rather
cold out in the waiting room.'

The other looked at her.

'You are very welcome,' he said. His
voice was low, and held a mournful note.

'If we're in the way at all, we can easily
wait outside,' Miss Frayle smiled at him
gratefully. The man made a deprecatory
gesture.

'You can wait here till the train comes
— looks like being a bit late. I shall be
grateful to you for your company.'

Doctor Morelle made no contribution
to the conversation, so she continued to
make the effort.

'I suppose this must be rather a lonely
job for you, isn't it?' she asked brightly,

15

'Lonely . . . ?' the man echoed, turning his sombre gaze on her and giving a queer, mirthless laugh. 'Why, you two are the first people I've spoken to since — since . . . ' His voice trailed off.

Watching him somewhat apprehensively, Miss Frayle thought his eyes misted over as he stared at the stove. Then he looked up and said with a twisted little smile: 'Yes, I don't have very much company.'

She suppressed a shiver. There was something about him that gave her an odd uneasy sensation. His face caught the light of the flame in the stove, which gave it a yellowed, parchment-like appearance. Deep lines ran down from his nose, and the corners of his mouth had a melancholy droop. There was a distorted look about it, accentuated by the trick of flickering light and shadow. His shoulders were rounded as if bent beneath some heavy load.

Outside, the wind continued to howl round the station, rattling the doors and occasionally lifting a loose sheet of the corrugated iron roof. The atmosphere of

the warm room seemed to have under-
gone some inexplicable change. Miss
Frayle felt it had been brought about by
the arrival of the man who now stood
staring down at the stove with an
unseeing gaze. Although, by his appearance and manner he had awakened her
sympathy, yet at the same time she felt
there was something — well, something
queer about him. She wished the train
would come.

Doctor Morelle glanced up from his
book and eyed the man as he bent down
to tie a bootlace, which had come
undone. He noted the shabby trousers
and their frayed turn-ups, with a jagged
tear in one of them. Miss Frayle had also
observed the man's shabby appearance.
Poor man! she thought. He looked as if
he needed someone to look after him.
Perhaps that was it — she felt a surge of
sympathy towards him — he hadn't got
anybody. And then having to be in a
lonely spot like this; it was enough to
make anyone look depressed and strange.
All the same, she reflected, there was
something else about him, too —

She glanced at the Doctor, who was about to return to his book, when suddenly the man spoke.

'Of course I always come here on this night,' he was saying. 'It's very important . . . ' His voice trailed off once more. Again that queer look.

Doctor Morelle said condescendingly:

'Yes, one would imagine you get few trains stopping here.'

The other nodded absently. Then he went on in that low, mournful tone:

'I was late once, you see,' he said. 'Yes, late . . . I must never be late again.' He heaved a deep sigh and closed his eyes as if to shut out the sight of something he could not bear to see. Mouth agape and eyes wide behind her spectacles, Miss Frayle stared at him. The Doctor regarded him as if he might have been a specimen of some fauna possibly worthy of cursory study.

'What — what d'you mean?' Miss Frayle swallowed. There was a prickly sensation under her scalp.

'That was why it happened — my fault!' The hysterical note in the man's

18

voice rose and was interrupted as the gale carried to them the distant whistle of an approaching train. The man tensed at once, his eyes wild, his mouth working.

'The train!' he croaked. 'The train!'

While she goggled at him, Doctor Morelle calmly slipped his book in his pocket, murmuring half to himself: 'It would seem the — ah — gentleman had never witnessed the arrival of a locomotive before!'

But his sarcasm was lost upon the other. The man rushed to the door, and picking up the suitcase, turned to fling back at them:

'You don't understand,' he moaned, 'You don't understand . . . '

'What about our tickets?' Miss Frayle remembered to gasp. But the man ignored her. He gave a wild look towards the platform as the sound of the train drew rapidly nearer.

'The gates!' he cried. 'The level-crossing gates . . . ' And he was gone. The wind caught the door and slammed it after him.

Doctor Morelle regarded Miss Frayle

with a sardonic and enigmatic look. She goggled back at him and then started for the door as the train rumbled into the station. The Doctor followed her at a more leisurely pace.

As he joined her on the platform she gulped at him anxiously:

'What — what shall we do about the tickets?'

'I feel confident that little matter can be adjusted quite easily, either on the train or at the terminus,' he said. Adding, with a thin smile: 'Rest assured there is only a slight risk of your being arrested on a charge of travelling without one!'

As the train rumbled in, the platform seemed deserted. Miss Frayle looked in all directions while she stood hesitating at the open door of the first-class compartment into which Doctor Morelle had stepped. She followed him and heard the slamming of doors further along the train, and she looked out of the window. All there was to be seen, however, was the guard's green lamp half obscured by the falling snow. Came the shrill of a whistle and the train drew out of Telbury Halt.

She closed the window and huddled in a corner seat facing the Doctor.

He was complaining in acid tones:

'Why, when the train would appear to be particularly empty, did you urge me into a non-smoking compartment?'

She glanced at the notice on the window beside her.

'Oh, I'm so sorry,' she apologised quickly. 'I didn't see — I was so anxious about the tickets and wondering where that strange man had gone — '

He cut into her excuses.

'You may remain here if you prefer,' he snapped, rising and moving to the door that led to the corridor, 'but I shall seek more desirable accommodation.'

'I'll come with you, of course, Doctor!'

After the disturbing events she had experienced, the last thing she looked forward to was being left alone in the empty compartment. Her imagination would soon people the corners and the corridor outside with frightening apparitions. She hurried after Doctor Morelle. Thus it was that a few minutes later she followed him into a smoking

21

compartment where he had paused to stand and regard with saturnine amusement its only other occupant who was snoring rhythmically in a corner. It was Detective-Inspector Hood of Scotland Yard.

As she touched the Doctor's arm he turned and motioned her into the seat next to his. He sat down facing the detective.

'This is somewhat more agreeable,' he observed, taking out his cigarette case and lighting a Le Sphinx. He made no attempt to lower his voice particularly, and Miss Frayle frowned and indicated the sleeping figure opposite.

'Shush!' she whispered. 'You'll wake him!'

'That,' he replied, 'is precisely what I propose to do!'

And he leaned across and tapped the sleeper firmly upon his knee.

The other awoke with a snort.

'What the devil — !' he began, then his mouth opened with surprise as he recognised the Doctor. 'Well, I'll be — !'

'Indulging in a little beauty sleep?'

murmured Doctor Morelle, regarding the detective's homely features. Detective-Inspector Hood blinked at him owlishly, then he grinned slowly at Miss Frayle. He sat upright in his corner and began automatically to forage in his pockets for his pipe. He found it and stuck it between his teeth, saying, as he found a match:

'Well, it is nice to meet you! But where on earth did you spring from?'

'We boarded the train at Telbury Halt,' explained Doctor Morelle. 'Might I inquire what coincidental circumstance causes you to be travelling by the same locomotive?'

'Yes, fancy you being on the train, too!' put in Miss Frayle.

The other sucked noisily at his old briar, slowly expelled a great cloud of somewhat acrid smoke — he went in for a powerful tobacco — apologised as the Doctor twitched his nostrils in revulsion, and explained:

'Maywood,' he said.

'Maywood?' Miss Frayle said helpfully. 'Isn't that about twenty miles the other side of Telbury?'

The other nodded, and his face assumed a disgruntled expression.

'And what, might I further inquire,' murmured Doctor Morelle, 'lured you so far afield from the precincts of Scotland Yard?'

The detective grunted

'Dragged down there on a fool's errand!' he growled.

'Some petty crime, no doubt, beneath your august consideration?'

'Well, I wouldn't describe it as petty exactly. The local police had nabbed a fellow for housebreaking, you see. By all accounts he sounded as if he might be the member of a gang I suspect are being operated from London. Thought a chat with him might lead me in the right direction towards rounding the lot up. But I got to Maywood just an hour too late. He's escaped!'

'Oh!' said Miss Frayle sympathetically. She added with a smile: 'He might have waited for you!'

'Extremely annoying,' agreed Doctor Morelle sardonically. 'But then the criminal classes are inclined to exhibit a tendency towards a deplorable lack of any sense of etiquette!'

'H'm — may seem funny to you, but it didn't make me laugh! Half-an-hour with that chap would have saved me a lot of headaches. He could have given me quite a lot of information . . . ' And he clamped his jaw so hard on his pipe-stem Miss Frayle feared it might snap.

'But surely the police will recapture him?' she asked.

Detective-Inspector Hood shrugged glumly.

'May not be as easy as all that,' he grumbled. 'For one thing, it's pretty certain he's got an accomplice. Not only that, he's an expert at disguise. They call him 'Rubber Face' — Riley's his real name. And he's one of the smartest men in the country at that sort of thing!'

He chewed at his pipe, which had gone out, but made no effort to relight it. 'Taken all round,' he said, 'it's a damn nuisance!'

'Admittedly a somewhat aggravating outcome for you,' the Doctor conceded.

The train drew into a station. Several

bumps and jarring noises occurred as it was attached to another train waiting, and then the journey was resumed.

'Non-stop to London now,' the detective explained.

'I won't be sorry to get there either!' breathed Miss Frayle in thankful anticipation. She had not altogether recovered from the earlier events of the evening. The warmth and security of the house in Harley Street was something she looked forward to.

Hood glanced at her and then at the Doctor, with a look of interrogation:

'Why, hasn't it been a nice change for you?' he queried. 'I mean yours wasn't a business trip — or was it?'

Miss Frayle at once started to launch into an account of what had occurred on their way to the station and at Telbury Halt itself. She had hardly begun, however, when she was interrupted by the corridor door sliding open. They looked up to see an old lady standing there rather uncertainly.

'I do hope you won't mind me coming in here,' she apologised in a thin, quavering voice. 'I'm a bit nervous — and I don't like travelling alone, especially at night.'

'Of course not,' Miss Frayle reassured her at once, while Hood rose with alacrity, took the suitcase she was carrying and placed it carefully on the rack.

Rewarding them with a grateful glance and a murmured word of thanks, the old lady seated herself in the corner opposite Miss Frayle, folding her hands primly on her lap. She seemed very slight and worn looking, and with a tiny sigh closed her eyes wearily. Miss Frayle studied her anxiously for a moment, then went on with the story which the newcomer's entrance had interrupted.

' . . . and when the strange man heard the train coming he shouted something about the gates — he was almost crazy with excitement — and rushed out.'

'Gates? What gates?' The Scotland Yard man who had been listening with amused interest suddenly shot out the query.

She blinked at him.

'Why — why, the level-crossing gates, of course.'

'What d'you mean?'

Something in his tone caused Doctor Morelle, who had returned again to his book, to look up sharply. Miss Frayle was goggling at the other who was eyeing her now with a puzzled frown.

'There isn't a crossing at Telbury Halt,' he said, sucking noisily at his pipe. He added decisively: 'It's a *bridge*'.

She stared at him. 'Bri-bridge?' she stammered, 'what do you mean?'

The Doctor's narrowed gaze fastened itself on the detective. He made no comment. Miss Frayle shook her head in bewilderment.

'Are you sure?'

'Positive,' he answered her. 'Noticed it going down. And as we came back tonight. Remember it distinctly.'

'But the porter? Those were his very words — ' she persisted, 'about the level-crossing. We both heard him, didn't we, Doctor Morelle?' And she turned to him for corroboration.

The Doctor, who had lit a Le Sphinx, blew out a spiral of cigarette-smoke thoughtfully. The Detective-Inspector glanced at

Miss Frayle, then at him:

'Perhaps you only dreamt it?' he suggested genially.

'Though Miss Frayle might conceivably have been asleep at the time,' said the Doctor, 'it is difficult very often to know with certainty when exactly she is *awake* — I certainly was in possession of my full faculties. Furthermore,' he went on, 'it is hardly within the bounds of possibility that both of us had we been somnolent would have experienced a dream identical in all its features.'

Hood was obviously impressed by the Doctor's pompous verbosity. He was about to ask further questions when the old lady opened her eyes and leaned forward.

'If you will pardon me for interrupting your conversation,' she said tentatively in a quavering voice. 'I think I might explain why the man spoke to you as he did about the level-crossing, although there is, in fact, a bridge there — I could not help overhearing what you were saying,' she added with a little apologetic smile.

Hood gestured with his pipe, and said

with an air of finality:

'There you are!'

'Telbury Halt used to have gates,' the old lady proceeded in thin, wavering tones. 'And it was the duty of the station-master — he was porter and booking-clerk as well — to open the gates for the train to pass through.' She paused, as if the exertion of speaking taxed her strength, then went on: 'But about five years ago — on a Sunday night it was — '

'It's Sunday tonight!' gasped Miss Frayle, her eyes wide, staring at the old lady in fascinated apprehension. The other nodded:

'Yes, I know,' she said quietly, 'but on this night I am speaking of five years ago, something happened to delay the poor man as he went to operate the gates. He reached them too late!' Her voice sank into a whisper that could hardly be heard. 'The train crashed through them and he was killed. Oh, it was a terrible business . . . ' She shook her head. 'Poor man, poor man . . . '

There was a long silence, then Miss Frayle gulped:

'You — you mean that — that the man we saw tonight — the man who rushed to open the gates — you mean he was — it was a — ?' She couldn't finish the question, becoming speechless with fright as the full implication of the other's story hit her.

The old lady nodded slowly. 'Everybody knows there is a bridge at Telbury Halt now. It was built soon after the accident.'

Miss Frayle turned her horrified gaze upon Doctor Morelle, who was leaning back in a relaxed attitude, his eyes closed. Without opening them, he puffed a spiral of cigarette smoke upwards.

Detective-Inspector Hood scratched his chin.

'Well, well!' he said, his eyebrows drawn together. 'What d'you make of that, Doctor Morelle?'

The lowered eyelids condescended to flicker open for a moment and he bent their sardonic gaze upon the detective. Then they closed again, and his only reply to the question was another puff of cigarette-smoke.

'H'm . . . I've come up against some queer characters in my time,' ruminated the detective, 'but you two have certainly got something on me there!' He chuckled. 'I've never had the pleasure of saying 'hello' to a ghost!'

Miss Frayle shivered at the remembrance. 'That is,' Hood added judiciously, 'if it was a spook.'

'Oh, other people have seen him,' the old lady said with conviction. 'He appears only once a year — on this particular night, of course — and anyone who knows about it keeps away from the station at this time on the anniversary of the awful accident.'

'I expect they do!' Miss Frayle said fervently. She shivered again. 'I wish we'd known.'

'Oh well,' Hood said cheerfully, 'it doesn't seem to have done you much harm!'

The old lady had fallen silent in her corner. Her head was sunk on her shoulder as if she had fallen asleep. The detective gave her a sympathetic look and then turned to the Doctor who was sitting more upright, a speculative gaze directed towards the woman.

'How do you come to be travelling by train, Doctor? I thought you got around by car?'

Doctor Morelle looked at him slowly, and then proceeded to give a brief explanation of the abandoning of his car.

'You haven't told the Inspector about that strange man who overtook us while we were waiting in the snow and drove off before you could ask him for help,' Miss Frayle reminded him. 'And there was that muffled figure in the back of his car — ' A sudden thought struck her, and she turned, wide-eyed, to the detective. 'Why, it might have been the escaped prisoner you're looking for!'

The other glanced at her sharply.

'You mean Riley?'

'Yes,' she said excitedly. 'You said he had an accomplice.'

Hood shot a look at the Doctor whose eyes had narrowed thoughtfully.

'It is not impossible that there is a grain of probability in what Miss Frayle suggests,' he conceded. 'Do you know if the car went on to Telbury Halt?' the Scotland Yard man asked.

Miss Frayle was about to answer eagerly, but the Doctor spoke first.

'To judge from tyre-tracks in the snow outside the station, that would seem to be indicated.'

Miss Frayle goggled at him. 'Oh, you did notice them?' she said.

He gave her a supercilious smile. To the other he went on:

'I compared them with the tyre-tracks which led from the spot where the car had pulled alongside mine.'

'Yet you saw no one at the station?'

'Only the ghost,' breathed Miss Frayle. 'Perhaps — perhaps he'd scared them away.'

'Never mind that,' the Detective-Inspector waved aside the idea. 'Where did the car get to? That's the point.'

'That remains to be ascertained,' observed the Doctor. 'Unfortunately it would have been impossible to note the vehicle's registration number inasmuch as the plate had become obscured by snow.'

'Pity. Though if it was Riley I don't

suppose getting the number would have helped much. He'd abandon the car as soon as he could.'

Doctor Morelle nodded in agreement.

'How awful if it really was him and he's got away,' put in Miss Frayle.

The other clicked his tongue. 'Pity. However, I'll have a call put out as soon as I get to London. We'll rope 'em in all right.' He relit his pipe and puffed at it confidently. Miss Frayle looked across at the other occupant of the compartment. Her eyes were closed.

Presently they steamed into the terminus. While Miss Frayle helped the old lady to her feet, Detective-Inspector Hood rose to lift down her suitcase. At the same time the Doctor was reaching for his luggage.

The woman's expressions of gratitude were abruptly cut short by a rather surprising mishap.

The Doctor was always extremely assured in his actions, but apparently an unexpected jerk of the train as it drew to a standstill with a final application of brakes caused him to let the end of his suitcase slip. A corner of it caught the old lady sharply on the side of the head. It was not a heavy blow, but sufficient to knock her hat — and the wig underneath — askew. Hood had swung round, startled by the old lady's somewhat unladylike exclamation, and found himself staring into a face that was, to him, familiar.

''Rubber Face' Riley!' he grunted.

'The ghost!' cried Miss Frayle simultaneously.

The wolf in sheep's clothing tried to make a dash for it, but Doctor Morelle obliged by neatly tripping him, followed by the Detective-Inspector sitting heavily on the man's chest.

★　★　★

Some time later, as he accompanied Doctor Morelle and Miss Frayle back from Scotland Yard to Harley Street in a police-car, Detective-Inspector Hood was saying:

'Yes . . . that was Riley all right you saw in the back of the car. He and the other

36

chap — we hope to get him shortly — had stolen it, only to find the petrol in the tank wouldn't take them far. They were afraid to risk stopping for a fresh supply — might have attracted attention — so they decided to try their luck at the railway station. They knocked out the man in charge and locked him in the parcels-office. Riley borrowed his cap, in case anybody else came along. His pal pushed off. Riley intended to board the train unobserved. That was why he tried to scare you off. But, unfortunately for him, you didn't scare so easily!'

Doctor Morelle smiled bleakly. He said: 'In order that he might enter the train unseen by us? That was his object, I presume, in pretending he had to attend to the gates?'

Hood nodded, and added: 'He found an empty compartment, drew the blinds, and made himself up as an old lady.'

'But why did he deliberately come into our compartment?' asked Miss Frayle, puzzled. 'He must have realised who you were?'

'Typical of Riley. He guessed the

stations would be watched for him, as in fact they were, and was afraid he might be a bit conspicuous on his own. Some sharp-eyed policeman might have spotted that 'old lady' rig-out. But by deliberately tacking himself on to us, he hoped he'd disarm any suspicion. Of course, when I spoilt his earlier yarn to you about the level-crossing gates at Telbury Halt, he thought up his ghost story to cover his tracks.'

'I must say he carried off both parts very well,' said Miss Frayle, not without a hint of admiration in her voice.

'He would appear to have missed his vocation,' murmured the Doctor. 'I should imagine he could appear with some success on the music-hall stage!'

'Perhaps you can persuade him to try it as a new career — when he comes out of gaol!' Hood suggested with a grin.

Doctor Morelle condescended to smile thinly at the pleasantry.

'Yes. If it hadn't been for that little accident,' the Detective-Inspector mused, 'he'd have walked past the barrier with us as easy as kiss-your-hand. I'd have carried his suitcase, and you, Miss Frayle, would've called him a taxi!'

Doctor Morelle lit a Le Sphinx with a sardonic smile twitching at the corners of his mouth.

'I think I may say that both those eventualities would have been unlikely,' he said.

'What d'you mean, Doctor?' queried Miss Frayle.

'Merely that as a result of elementary observation I perceived that the end of a gentleman's trouser-leg, presumably hurriedly packed, had become caught in the lid of his suitcase,' he murmured in an elaborately casual tone. 'Moreover, the turn-up in question had suffered a tear — ' He paused, and then went on, ' — exactly similar to the tear in the trouser-leg of the — ah — 'ghost of Telbury Halt'!'

Miss Frayle goggled at him from behind her spectacles.

'You — you mean — ?' she gasped.

'Well, I'll be — !' Hood could find no words to express his surprise.

'You sloshed him with your suitcase

deliberately!' Miss Frayle blurted out in excited astonishment and admiration.

The police-car was drawing up outside the house in Harley Street as Doctor Morelle replied through a cloud of cigarette smoke:

'Though you have hardly taken the exact words out of my mouth, my dear Miss Frayle, you have nevertheless succeeded in interpreting my implied meaning.'

2

The Case of the Man in the Squared Circle

Despite her timorous and sensitive temperament Miss Frayle on the whole, enjoyed working for Doctor Morelle. At least her duties had the advantage of constant change and variety, and they took her into strange and fascinating places. Through the Doctor she had met many interesting people. At the same time there was a great deal of routine matter to which she had to attend, and she could evince very little interest in these mundane tasks. It afforded her infinitesimal solace that sociology and psychological research was, to the Doctor, more interesting than the most thrilling encounters with murderers, malcontents, blackmailers and poison-pen writers — that sordid gentry of avarice-ridden social misfits who flit like murky shadows across

41

the life of anyone engaged in crime detection.

She realised full well that the mysteries of the subconscious, to Doctor Morelle, were more breathtakingly exciting than the most complex real-life 'who done it.' That the most glamorous and colourful crook interested him less than the retrogressive stages of dementia praecox. By bitter experience she knew that when the Doctor was engaged in such theoretical research, his preoccupation with the subject would enable him to work untiringly until the small hours of the morning, completely unmindful of the fact that she did not share such interest to that extent. Such things were beyond her mental powers, and when she made foolish mistakes in her note taking, he would become loquaciously condemnatory of her limited intelligence.

It was with a heartfelt groan, therefore, that Miss Frayle greeted Doctor Morelle's announcement one morning that they would be devoting the next two weeks to intensive research activities.

She tried to hide her boredom by

assuming what she hoped was a 'poker-face'. This did not, however, escape his lynx-like observation.

'Your features possess the fixity of expression of the manic depressive,' he snapped. 'Am I to assume you do not relish the prospect of our research work?'

'Oh, I daresay it'll be a nice change,' she said absently, and resigned herself to days of searching for references in thick verbose volumes, and the inscribing of the Doctor's endless notes. Actually she need have had no fears of *ennui*, because the research work was fated to be, for Miss Frayle, the most interesting sequence of duties she had ever undertaken.

'I am writing a thesis,' the Doctor continued, pacing the study with long raking strides, 'and the title is: 'Hedonism and the Masses.'

Miss Frayle looked up brightly. 'Hedonism? Let me see Doctor — isn't that the pursuit of pleasure?'

'Correct, Miss Frayle.' He gave a half-derisive smile. 'A subject, I presume, well within your limited sphere! This is not a task that I personally relish, however. Nevertheless, the scientist must, for the sake of humanity, forget his own squeamishness. I regret deeply that our research work will take us into numerous sordid places — '

'What places, for instance?'

'To the kinema, no doubt — ' He gave the word its abstruse Greek pronunciation. 'To the theatre, and even to the subterranean establishments where moronic people congregate nocturnally.'

'You mean nightclubs?' and it was all she could do to prevent herself clapping her hands in excitement. 'Now I'll be able to wear my evening frock.'

Surprisingly he inclined his head in agreement.

'Throughout these researches it will indubitably assist me if you display your normal reactions towards these various entertainments,' he said weightily. 'Since you, my dear Miss Frayle, are typical of the more cretinous section of the public, your reactions will, I imagine, be representative of the masses. For once therefore, I shall strive *not* to curb your indiscriminate enthusiasms.'

'It's going to be thrilling,' she enthused. 'It'll take me out of myself.'

Her observation prompted him to write one word on his notepad: '*Escapism*'.

The Doctor's coldly analytical and often sweepingly denunciatory criticisms of entertainments which are meant to be accepted only superficially afforded considerable amusement to Miss Frayle in the next few days. She had accompanied him to a mammoth Hollywood film, packed with drama, romance, song, and technicolour. On their return the Doctor had dictated:

'The kinema is patently the refuge of the physically lonely and the spiritually lost. The relaxation which the masses apparently attain by sitting in a darkened interior would indicate that they are seeking subconsciously to return to the pre-natal state.'

After he had accompanied Miss Frayle to the first night of a society comedy, he dictated:

'The appeal of the theatre would appear to be purely exhibitionistic — both on the part of the players, who

45

cavort and display themselves in a hysterically inspired manner — and on the part of the audience who draw attention to themselves by arriving tardily for the performance, and who preen themselves in a vulgar finery during the intermissions when the illuminations are increased apparently with the sole object that the patrons may exhibit themselves with greater abandon in the confidence that they can be observed.'

Of nightclubs and people who sleep during the day and play all night, he observed sententiously:

'Garish establishments exist where neurotic persons may set the wheels of evolution turning backwards. These people perform licentious gyrations to cacophonies that have primeval rhythm. Such people, no doubt, through childhood traumas, have cause to fear the world of daylight. Psychologically they are retrograding to the Dark Age.'

Indeed, when the *maitre* of an expensive nightclub had obsequiously bowed Doctor Morelle and Miss Frayle to a table on the edge of the narrow dance floor, Miss Frayle could scarcely believe she was not dreaming. While the Doctor toyed distastefully with a shrivelled Lobster Neuborg, she observed him closely. With rude directness he was watching one group of merry-makers after another, as though he was seeking to read their thoughts. Some solitary and peroxided females quite reasonably imagined his interest to be other than academic — and Miss Frayle shuddered as she saw girls ogling him shamelessly. A dance-hostess had even sidled up to their table quite brazenly and, at his request, the creature had actually joined them — though she had quickly left when she realised the Doctor was more interested in her subconscious maladjustments than her physical charms!

Next day, however, it was with regret that Miss Frayle heard the Doctor state that the research was almost concluded.

'To complete my thesis,' he announced, flicking the ash off his Le Sphinx, 'it only remains for us to visit a display of fisticuffs.'

'Oh, a boxing match!' she translated.

'Precisely, my dear Miss Frayle.' A thin smile quirked his lips. 'I relish this task more than the others. Pugilism can be a manly art for the participants, though the appeal for the onlookers must, for the most part, be grossly sadistic or, in your language, Miss Frayle, the delight in the infliction of pain.'

She reached for the telephone. 'Would you like me to book ringside seats for some match?' she asked helpfully.

'That will not be necessary.' He pulled an envelope from his wallet. 'Fortuitously, an acquaintance of mine, Mr. William Royston, who is a coach at the Fencing Club which I attend, has procured me the means of admission to an arena by the name of Ringland. Mr. Royston appeared anxious for me to attend this display, since his young son is one of the leading participants.'

As they set out to Ringland on the following Saturday night, Miss Frayle took a notebook and pencil, so that she could write down any notes which the Doctor would suggest as he observed different details. On the other evenings of the week (the Doctor had discovered) the great barn of a place was given over to popular dances, concerts, political meetings and so forth; Saturdays were the only days devoted to the science and noble art of professional pugilism.

Such apparently was the lure of the roped arena, so strong a hold did our modern gladiators have upon the hearts and pockets of the public, that on 'fight night' all roads seemed to lead to the large, unhandsome building where programmes always promised action and thrills, and prices were cheap.

On Saturday night Ringland was sure to be jammed. Packed to suffocation with noisy, enthusiastic 'fans', and a good time was had by all, with the possible exception — or so the Doctor deduced — of those performers in the ring unfortunate enough to catch a heavy beating from their opponents.

Though even they might be seen again in the same ring upon some subsequent occasion, gamely taking another mauling, or this time, perhaps, handing one out to the other fellow.

Of the thousands who packed the hall, Doctor Morelle was the only one who wasn't tensed eagerly for the fights. Through lowered eyelids he peered across the smoke-filled auditorium with less interest than if he were observing bacteria through a microscope. Occasionally he bent to one side or the other to eavesdrop on the conversation of others. This was purely in the interests of scientific research. The Doctor listened, analytically, to two evident sports fans who were talking enthusiastically on his right.

'Nothink like a nice clean scrap, there ain't,' one of the men was saying. 'Mind you, it's boxin' I wants to see. None o' these sluggin' heavyweights what moves around each other like a couple of elephants and ties themselves up in clinches all the time.'

The man next to him nodded heavily.

'I agree,' he said. 'Give me the quick and clever ones. Boys with science and skill.'

'Like this one 'ere,' the first man gestured with his pipe towards the ring, where in the corner nearest them two seconds were ministering to a young boxer.

One of the white-sweatered men was grizzle-haired, but this seemed to be the only evidence that he was past middle age, for he was slim and as active looking as the youngster he was attending and to whom he bore a strong resemblance.

'That person is William Royston,' Doctor Morelle informed Miss Frayle. 'The younger man will be his son. Rather an exceptionally finely developed youth, do you not agree?'

'He looks awfully strong,' she nodded. She saw the young man smiling across to some friends. 'He's good-looking, too. I hope he doesn't get hurt.'

The Doctor again switched his attention from Miss Frayle's verbal commonplaces to his neighbours' more colourful comments.

'Yes, he's a smart kid, all right,' one of them said. 'A case of like father like son — though, of course, he's a long way off what the old man was in his prime.'

'Only just twenty the boy is, y'know,' the other was saying.

'His dad's bringin' him along slow and easy-like. Got great 'opes in 'im, 'is dad 'as.'

'He certainly has the makings of a champ,' observed the other.

'And he couldn't be in better hands.'

'No more 'e couldn't, and that's a fact,' the first man agreed.

He glanced sharply at Doctor Morelle, and whispered loud enough for him to hear, ' 'Ere, I say oo's this nosey geezer 'oo keeps staring at us? Is 'e a friend o' yourn?'

The second man glanced at Doctor Morelle:

'Strewth, no bloomin' fear!'

Quickly the Doctor diverted his gaze across the ropes to the man in the sweater who was busily engaged in massaging the boy's legs.

The Doctor knew that it was the elder man's dream that one day his youngster would hold the middleweight title as he himself had once held it. Royston had often spoken about the boy to patrons of the Fencing Club. Carefully he had nursed the boy along, mindful of the disaster that overtakes many a promising young boxer through being matched with men for whom they are too inexperienced and raw.

Bill Royston wisely kept his boy back, picking each opponent for him with a shrewd eye as to his value as a 'trial horse'.

Thus for tonight's fight, Sonny Royston was matched against one 'Iron' Kelly, a battle-scarred veteran possessed of little real boxing skill, but wily and cunning through the bitter experience of scores of fights, and full of all the cruder tricks of his trade.

Against such an antagonist, a young boxer, provided he knew enough to keep out of the way of the other's destructive but erratic punches, could learn much in ring generalship and ringcraft, and at the same time stand a good chance of scoring enough points to gain him the verdict.

The seconds were out and the boxers were limbering up in their corners. The referee gave them instructions; they touched gloves and the fight was on. It was uneventful enough for the first few rounds, though the fourth round was lively, and ended to roars of applause from the spectators whom young Royston had delighted with his skill and speed. 'Iron' Kelly, on the other hand, having earned a number of cautions from the referee for holding and shady tactics generally, had received the crowd's heartily expressed disapprobation.

Sonny Royston had clearly shown he was a true chip off the old block by his cleverness and boxing ability. His attractive style, together with his fair hair and smiling blue eyes, as compared with the rushing, reckless methods of his heavy-featured opponent, had caught the imagination of the crowd.

He had been scoring repeatedly with a beautifully timed left and was ahead on points. Provided he continued to evade the other's vicious, but ill-aimed blows — and his footwork had so far kept him out of danger — the fight was his.

Doctor Morelle again eavesdropped. He heard his neighbour saying:

'His style's very reminiscent of his father's. I remember when I saw the old chap fight the coloured chap — what's his name — ?'

The man went off into a reminiscence of one of Bill Royston's famous fights.

Suddenly Doctor Morelle's attention was diverted by a man who rose from his seat by the ringside and with a smile at his blonde companion, made his way towards the exit.

'A singularly cretinous type — both the man and the woman companion,' the Doctor diagnosed. 'Typical of the unhealthy section of the parasitic community who watch sport and never participate.'

He noted with distaste that the man was short and wasp-waisted, that his wide shoulders in his too slickly cut suit gave him a deformed appearance. Hatchet-faced and of a greyish pallor, the man pulled on a pearl-grey trilby, slanting it over one eye.

As the man swaggered past, Doctor Morelle noticed that two pink ticket counterfoils were stuck incongruously in the hatband. Although the weather was warm and the atmosphere in the Ring-land was stifling, the man, strangely enough, was wearing gloves that were buttoned round his wrists.

The man next to Doctor Morelle said in awed tones: 'That's Joe Girroti — one of the Girotti boys. A proper race-course crook!'

All this was singularly interesting to the Doctor. Already in his index-like mind he was formulating the meticulously worded notes that he would dictate to Miss Frayle on their return that evening.

He felt a tap on his shoulder and he looked up to see Detective-Inspector Hood of Scotland Yard smiling down at him in his homely way.

'So this is where the great Doctor seeks his recreation,' the Inspector grinned widely. 'I've heard about cabinet ministers bricklaying, and poets planting potatoes, and I guess you too — '

'My presence here is solely in the interest of sociological research,' Doctor Morelle interjected with a cold smile

The other winked at Miss Frayle. 'That's what the vicar said when he was caught talking to a coupla girls in Piccadilly!' He shook the Doctor's hand warmly. 'It's nice to see you again.' He foraged in his pocket for his pipe, and drew out a slab of candy, which he presented gallantly to Miss Frayle.

'Last time we met was at Telbury Halt, if you remember,' he reminisced. 'I was chasing a gang of house-breakers, and you and the Doctor were of invaluable assistance.'

Doctor Morelle lit a Le Sphinx. 'It was I who elucidated the mystery for you, was it not?' he remarked innocently, and he added with a smile: 'Am I to assume that since you are wearing your cylindrical headgear, sartorially known as a *bowler*, that you are here on official business?'

'I'm just keeping my eyes on the boys,' the Inspector replied, sucking noisily at his acrid-smelling briar. 'You get all sorts at a prizefight.'

'Would you be particularly maintaining a watch upon one Mr. Joseph Girotti?'

'Well, I was,' Hood admitted with a smile. 'Seems I can't keep anything from you, Doctor! Girotti's a pickpocket among other things. He's fly enough to wear gloves as an alibi whenever he spies any of the police. Nasty bit of work he is!'

He raised his bowler affably. 'Hope to see you again; must get back to my seat before the next round starts. Enjoy yourselves!'

At that moment the bell rang for the fifth round. With a nod as his father gave him a last-minute word of counsel, young Royston came out of his corner to meet a devastating onslaught from 'Iron' Kelly.

Leastways, the attack was intended to be devastating, but Sonny slipped away from the whirl of fists like a shadow, poking his left hand into the other's face with irritating frequency as he did so. Kelly paused for a moment, baffled, then with a ferocious scowl, he charged in again.

This time he slipped and fell upon one knee. With a cheery grin Royston moved forward and helped him to his feet, stepping back to give the man time to steady himself.

The sporting action brought a roar of approval from the fans. Kelly, however, seemed strongly to resent the friendly gesture, for he immediately rushed forward and swung a mighty right that caught the youngster well below the belt. There was a howl of rage from the crowd. 'Foul! Dirty! Kick him out, ref!'

The referee seemed to have been unsighted, however, and the fight continued, Kelly doing his utmost to barge in close to the shaken youngster and administer a knockout.

Crowding him hard against the ropes, he threw in punches from every angle and it looked as if only a miracle could save his victim from sinking beneath the storm. Pandemonium broke out in the hall. Doctor Morelle half stood in his seat so that he could watch with better advantage this astonishing display of mass hysteria — unique even in the casebook of Kraft-Ebbing. Miss Frayle clung on to his arm, terrified free fights might break out among the spectators and she might lose the new hat she had bought for the occasion. Meanwhile the two dramatic white figures battled beneath the blazing arc lamps. Doctor Morelle observed poor Bill Royston, his face grey with anxiety, crying out to his son to fall into a clinch, and hang on. A section of the crowd found themselves echoing the trainer's frantic appeal, with electric suddenness — which the Doctor could only account for as a phenomenon of mass telepathy.

'Clinch, Sonny!' came the cries. 'Clinch!'

But Sonny appeared unable to follow the advice that was now being offered to him from all sides. He lay across the ropes, his protective left shoulder dropped to expose his vulnerable jaw and his adversary drew back his right glove to administer the *coup de grace*.

A mammoth groan came from a hundred throats — and then with a sudden tautening of Sonny Royston's lithe body, the boy's left arm straightened out to smash with terrific force against the other's jaw that he had left exposed in his anxiety to deliver the finishing blow.

Kelly stood swaying for a second, his eyes glazing over then dropped flat on his face.

The voice of the referee, as he began to count, was swamped by the thunder of applause and the ear-piercing whistles of delight that filled the building. The counting-out was, however, a pure formality; 'Iron' Kelly never looked like moving inside ten minutes, let alone ten seconds.

Miss Frayle found herself joining wildly in the cheering. She caught the Doctor's mocking gaze, and blushed slightly.

'It would appear that you are quite appreciative of the pugilistic science,' he observed calmly.

'I got carried away, Doctor,' she smiled. 'I'm glad the good-looking young man won. He deserved to.'

'Indeed, yes. He certainly displayed more science than his adversary.'

'I bet his father's proud of him.'

'And justifiably so.' The Doctor rose, and pushed through a throng of people. So magnetic and compelling was his personality that they made room for him immediately.

'Wait for me, Doctor!' called Miss Frayle, fearing she would lose him in the crush.

'Hurry then!'

She caught up with him, and breathlessly tried to keep pace.

'Where are we going to?' she panted.

'To the dressing room. Courtesy behoves us to congratulate the victor, and his worthy parent.'

'Aren't we going to see the rest of the fights?' she queried eagerly. She had never believed that she would enjoy a boxing match so much.

'We may later.'

They pushed down a corridor to a door, on which was chalked the name 'Sonny Royston,' and Doctor Morelle rapped sharply. He turned to Miss Frayle:

'It would be advisable for you to remain outside for the moment,' he told her shortly.

He pushed inside the door, and was immediately greeted by Bill Royston.

'Evening, Doctor Morelle,' the trainer smiled genially. 'Glad you could get along. My lad wants to meet you. He's got into his clothes already. It's a girl he's rushing off to meet.'

Doctor Morelle shook hands with the modest young boxer. He then summoned Miss Frayle and presented her to Sonny Royston. Her eyes were limpid with admiration behind her spectacles.

'He's courting, is Sonny,' Bill Royston went on proudly. 'Not that that's a bad thing for a boxer when it's the right girl.' His genial smile faded for a moment. 'But it's a rum business. He has to court on the sly — '

'Rather restrictive, I should imagine,' the Doctor observed.

'You're right! You see, his young lady's Kitty Burgess — only daughter of Hal Burgess, the man who promotes the boxing here. I suppose Hal has seen so many boxers become punch-drunk or lose their money he doesn't want his daughter running round with one. Her dad won't allow 'em to meet now he knows they're in love with each other. Won't let her even watch the boy fight.'

'That's right, Doctor Morelle,' Sonny put in over his shoulder as he carefully knotted his tie in a cracked mirror. 'He told me Kitty wasn't for a struggling fighter. Yesterday, that was, when I asked him if we could get engaged. Showed me the door and said I wasn't to see her again.'

The young boxer laughed amiably.

'Silly old chump! 'Course it's made no difference to Kitty and me — only now we have to meet on the sly, which we don't like really, and she's not allowed to come and watch me fight. She's waiting for me now in the café across the road.'

'Good for her!' Miss Frayle said feelingly, and Sonny grinned widely at her. Then he said to his father: 'Wonder if her dad saw me win tonight? Might make him change his mind.'

'Try him and see,' said the elder man with a grim quirk on his lips.

His son nodded. 'Perhaps not,' he said.

'Better wait till you're champ,' somebody laughed. There were a number of other happily smiling people in Royston's dressing room. 'Then he'll give you his daughter — if you'll agree to fight exclusively at Ringland for him!'

There was general amusement at this remark, for Hal Burgess was noted for his shrewd business acumen and his ability to strike a hard bargain. After receiving further hearty slaps on the back and renewed congratulations on his praise-worthy victory, the young boxer hurried off to keep his clandestine appointment.

The dressing room emptied quickly when he had gone, nearly everybody returning to the auditorium, for there was still some boxing to be seen, until only Doctor Morelle, Miss Frayle, and Bill Royston remained.

Miss Frayle was on tenterhooks to get back to the bouts.

'It's a bit of a worry about Kitty and Sonny,' Bill Royston was saying to Doctor Morelle.

'It does seem somewhat unsatisfactory.'

'It is.' Bill Royston scratched his grizzle-head in puzzlement. 'You see, I was pleased about him becoming genuinely attached to the girl, who's a nice kid, and him looking forward to marrying her. After all, the boy's only human and it was much better for him to be really serious over someone like Kitty, than to be chasing after raggle-taggle no-goods.'

'Perhaps it'll all come right in the end, Mr. Royston,' Miss Frayle put in banally.

'I hope so,' he said feelingly. 'If it all

fizzles out, as it might with Burgess forbidding her to see him, I'll be worried Sonny may start running a bit wild.' He scratched his head again despairingly — 'I wish his mother was here sometimes to give me a hand,' he said.

Bill Royston's wife had died several years previously.

Doctor Morelle turned to Miss Frayle with a bland smile. 'No doubt Miss Frayle would be able to give you sterling advice,' he murmured. 'She suffers from repressed maternal instincts.'

Royston looked at her hopefully.

'What do you make of it, miss?' he asked.

She thought for a moment. 'Speaking as a woman,' she began, 'I don't think Kitty Burgess is going to stop being in love with your son, Mr. Royston, just because her father tells her to. Why it'll make her love him all the more. I'm sure of that. Girls of today know their own minds. Sooner or later, Mr. Burgess will have to give in.'

'I hope so — and without any ill-feeling,' Royston said sincerely.

The Doctor lit a Le Sphinx casually. He was not to know that at that moment Hal Burgess lay dead in his office not far away. He might possibly have known nothing about it, except when the promoter's death had become news, had he not chanced to meet a sturdy, thick-set individual wearing a bowler hat going up to the offices that lay over the main entrance hall. This was a little while later when, deciding not to stay to see the last bout of the evening he left Royston and was on his way out with Miss Frayle.

'Doctor Morelle!' the man in the bowler hat hailed. 'I've been looking for you everywhere. Thought you'd left. I'd appreciate your help.'

The Doctor recognised again Detective-Inspector Hood of Scotland Yard.

'Another little mystery you wish me to elucidate?' he queried.

'Something like that,' the other nodded grimly. 'Someone's stuck a knife into someone else.' He blew a dark cloud of smoke from his strong-smelling briar. 'Don't ask me why, Doctor — I don't know yet.'

'Is — is it murder?' Miss Frayle stammered.

'I shouldn't be surprised. Suicides don't habitually stab themselves in the back — unless, of course, they happen to be contortionists, or something.'

Doctor Morelle dropped his cigarette and trod on it.

'Has the identity of the deceased been established?'

'Yes — it's Hal Burgess, the manager of this place.'

Miss Frayle started. She gulped: 'Hal Burgess — Kitty Burgess's father! Goodness, but this is terrible!'

The Scotland Yard man gave a grim smile. 'Murder usually is,' he remarked, and began to climb up the stairs, calling over his shoulder, 'the body's up here, Doctor.'

They entered an office near the head of the stairway to find a number of police officials already present. Miss Frayle remained in the doorway, too nervous to enter. The Doctor stared down at the shape that lay near the desk and was covered by a sheet.

His narrowed eyes shifted to where, on the desk, beside what was apparently the dead man's grey trilby, a knife was prominently placed upon a handkerchief. He observed the handkerchief was stained red. He removed his gaze from the unpleasant sight, and was eyeing the hat when he heard Hood say:

'Any idea how long ago death took place, Doctor?'

'Approximately half an hour ago. The right lung is punctured, the implement which killed him was evidently used with considerable force.'

Meanwhile Hood was surveying the knife on the desk with narrowed eyes. Beneath the glare of a powerful electric bulb, his ruddy features were grim and set. He examined the knife closely.

'Fingerprints seem clear enough,' he observed. 'Seems as though it's a straightforward case. Probably shan't have to take up your time after all.'

From what the Doctor was able to ascertain, it appeared that one of the boxing stewards calling at the office to check some point about the running of the programme had found the promoter dead, and had immediately searched for Detective-Inspector Hood, whom he had previously seen in the auditorium, so conspicuous was this amiable Scotland Yard man.

Inquiries had elicited that no suspicious person had been noticed in the vicinity of the office. But as the attention of everybody was engaged inside the hall, it would have been possible for someone to have come from almost any part of the building and make their way upstairs without attracting attention, or they could as easily have slipped in from the street. The motive for the crime was not robbery; the dead man's well-lined notecase was untouched.

Sounds that the last fight of the evening was over and the noise of the crowd leaving the building reached the office.

Doctor Morelle picked up his walking stick and beckoned to Miss Frayle.

'As the interception of the murderer would appear to be a foregone conclusion, Inspector, owing to the fingerprints,

I take it you will not require my assistance?'

'That's right. Sorry to have bothered you,' Hood declared. 'Good night, Doctor — good night, Miss.'

Outside the office door, Miss Frayle said:

'I've never known you to walk out on a case before, Doctor. Did you really believe that it's almost solved?' she asked quickly.

He tapped his walking stick on the concrete floor.

'On the contrary, my dear Miss Frayle,' he said enigmatically. 'I am quite confident that Detective-Inspector Hood will not be able to intercept the real perpetrator of the crime.'

'Then why don't you do something?'

'I intend so to do,' he replied evasively, and then snapped, 'as soon as you refrain from your banal interrogations!'

He hurried down the stairs, and stood surveying the people who streamed out of the more expensive seats. He was about to turn towards the exit when he perceived the individual whom he had been informed was Joe Girotti.

His blonde, flashily-dressed companion on his arm, he was swaggering through the crowd. He put on his hat with a dashing gesture, but instead of it slanting over his eyes it seemed to perch on the back of his black, shining head, and the girl looking up at it laughed as with a quick movement he removed it.

Doctor Morelle unexpectedly wheeled round and pulled Miss Frayle towards a telephone booth near the entrance.

'Kindly telephone the Fencing Club,' he directed, 'and ascertain the address of Mr. William Royston without delay.'

A question formed on her lips, but she stifled it when she saw the saturnine set of his feature in the half-light. Ten minutes later they were proceeding in a taxi to the Royston home. There seemed to be a long interval after Doctor Morelle had rung the bell before the door was opened to him by the elder Royston, whose face relaxed with obvious relief when he recognised his visitors.

'Thank heaven it's you, Doctor,' he exclaimed. 'You are the one person who

72

can help us. For a moment I thought it was the police.'

'So you, too, have a latent guilt complex,' the Doctor smiled mirthlessly.

Sonny Royston came into the room at that moment. He looked the picture of utter dejection.

'Shall I tell the Doctor, Dad?'

'Yes, go on, Sonny. He'll be able to tell us the best thing we can do.'

The young boxer hesitated, then he blurted out: 'It's Kitty's father. He's dead — murdered!'

'Of that I am cognisant,' the Doctor nodded. 'That is the reason I journeyed here. That reason and this — ' He handed Sonny a button. 'This belongs to you, I presume? I retrieved it from the late Mr. Burgess's office.'

Sonny Royston turned to his father helplessly. 'You see, Dad,' he cried, 'the police are going to think it was I who did it!'

'All right, son, take it easy,' said his father. Doctor Morelle stared at the boy piercingly, as though he was trying to make up his mind. Young Royston choked and then, his father's grip on his shoulder, proceeded more calmly. 'Remember tonight in the dressing room, Doctor, I joked about asking old Burgess if he'd seen me win my fight and wouldn't he change his mind about Kitty and me? Well, after I'd left you I suddenly thought perhaps after all it wouldn't be such a bad time to speak to him again about our engagement. So I decided to go up to his office before joining Kitty over at the café. There was no reply when I knocked, so I went in. He was on the floor and there was a knife in his back. Without thinking, I knelt down and pulled it out — ' He shuddered. 'It was horrible, and then some of the blood got on my hand and I wiped it off with my handkerchief. Suddenly I lost my head and rushed out.

'When I reached the street I realised I'd left my fingerprints on the knife. I remembered people knew he and I had quarrelled. I panicked absolutely and came home — I forgot all about poor Kitty — when I got here I burnt the handkerchief and then I waited for Dad.' He glanced at his father. 'You know I didn't do it, don't you?' he choked. 'You know that what I've told you is true?'

' 'Course I believe you,' said the elder man. He looked across at Doctor Morelle, his face drawn and harassed.

The Doctor walked across to the boy's side with a purposeful air.

'I must say I am constrained to believe you, young man — he began.'

'I believe you, too,' Miss Frayle burst in feelingly.

'It hardly seems consistent,' the Doctor continued, ignoring his assistant, 'that after you displayed such sportsmanship in the ring you would transfix anyone in the back.'

'All the same,' said Bill Royston after a moment, 'the fact that we all believe him doesn't mean to say that police will, does it? What ought we to do about it?'

'Surely you've got a clue, Doctor,' Miss Frayle insisted frenziedly, realising that Sonny Royston's freedom — and probably his life — depended on the Doctor elucidating this mystery.

'Regrettably, I fear I have no constructive suggestion to make at this juncture.'

He stretched out a hand to reach his hat, which he had placed on the table. Then, strangely, he turned it round in his hand, gazing at it with a sardonic smile. Suddenly he wheeled round. 'May I be permitted to amend my former statement? On the contrary, I can elucidate the crime, and in a few minutes put the police on to the true perpetrator.'

'Doctor, you're wonderful!'

It was Miss Frayle who said it, but the others in the room evidently thought the same, judging from the relief that came over their anxious faces.

'Now, young man, if you will kindly direct me to the telephone.'

A short while later found the Doctor on the telephone to Scotland Yard, speaking to Detective-Inspector Hood. The latter was working late on the checking up of the fingerprints found on the knife that had slain Burgess.

'What is it, Doctor?' Hood asked quickly. 'Found the murderer?'

'Your powers of deduction amaze me, because your assumption is quite correct.

If you will kindly assimilate the information I am about to give you . . . '

The Detective-Inspector acted upon Doctor Morelle's information forthwith, with the result that some time after midnight Joe Girotti opened the front door of his expensive flat to find himself face to face with Inspector Hood and a couple more formidable-looking officers.

At Scotland Yard he admitted to murdering Burgess — the promoter had refused to pay for his 'protection' (another name for blackmail which Girotti extorted from his victims under the threat of being beaten up by the 'boys').

Burgess had shown him the door, and the gang-leader, in a burst of rage, had waited until his back was turned and then attacked him with his knife.

The following day, Hood called at the house in Harley Street to thank Doctor Morelle for his assistance, and also to learn how he had so unerringly deduced the identity of the murderer.

'I observed what was to be the vital clue before the murder was actually committed,' the Doctor explained laconically. 'But, shall I say I observed it only subconsciously? You see, the real object of my presence at the prizefight was to gather impressions that would form a sociological subject. Not being cognisant of the fact that a murder was to be perpetrated, I was not searching for details. Briefly, I must have noticed two admission tickets fixed in the band of Girotti's headgear. The observation immediately passed into my subconscious, and then, in Burgess's office I perceived a hat on the table, very like Girotti's. Two tickets were also adhering to that hat.

'Later in the auditorium I perceived Girotti again, and I noticed then the headgear he now possessed did not appear to fit him properly — and he preferred not to wear it. Later, when interrogating Royston and his son, it occurred to me it was Burgess's hat Girotti had taken in error, leaving his own in the office. No doubt this happened in Girotti's haste to depart.'

'I see,' said Detective-Inspector Hood,

through a cloud of acrid tobacco smoke. 'But what was it suddenly brought these clues from your subconscious to your conscious mind, so to speak?'

Doctor Morelle chuckled sardonically. 'That occurred when I happened to reach for my headgear which was reposing on the Roystons' table. I observed that I, too, had inadvertently fixed the boxing arena admission tickets to my own hat, and had omitted to remove them.' He lit a Le Sphinx. 'And so you have a perfect example of how the subconscious can be brought into use in the elucidation of crime.'

'It sounds like Greek to me.'

Doctor Morelle walked towards the door. 'Now, Detective-Inspector, if you will bear with us, I wish to dictate to Miss Frayle my final notes on a thesis, entitled 'Hedonism and the Masses'.'

The Scotland Yard man grinned. 'Work! Work! Work!' he said. 'Don't you ever think of anything else, Doctor? Don't you ever think of — well, *pleasure*?'

3

The Case of the Spanish Sailor

Miss Frayle stood in the hotel porch and gazed rapturously across the grassy cliff to the grey line of the sea as dusk dimmed the bleak Cornish coastline.

'It's nice to be at the sea even in the middle of winter,' she told herself, and she took a deep breath of the keen air. Doctor Morelle had motored from Harley Street a few days previously to attend an old patient in whom he was particularly interested.

His professional visit was now ended, and he planned to return on the morrow. The Cornish fishing village, a favourite haunt of artists and fishermen, was deserted of visitors, and in the hotel the main dining room was closed. Nevertheless it had been rather a novelty for Miss Frayle and Doctor Morelle to have meals in a little private room where there was always a cheery blaze in the open brick fireplace.

A freshening wind stirred Miss Frayle's hair. She unwound the scarf from her neck and tied it round her head. Then, with the spontaneous joy of life, she ran down the little path to the edge of the cliff. Fifty feet below she saw a sandy bay, and the sea foaming against the yellow sand. She paused for a moment in the growing dusk. 'It would be a pity not to go down to the beach and get some sand in my shoes,' she thought. 'Goodness knows when we'll come down to the sea again.'

Impulsively she began to scramble down the narrow path, congratulating herself that she was wearing sensible-heeled shoes. A cold, freshening wind whipped the colour in her cheeks, and gulls wheeling overhead, cackled and laughed as though to share her feelings of happiness and invigoration. She leapt the last two feet from a small rock on to the sand, and walked briskly along the small beach. She paused at a rocky pool, removed her gloves and dipped a finger in the cold water. She put the finger to her lips. 'Salty!' she pronounced, and she giggled at her own foolishness.

The wind veered round from the sea, and flung a fine spume over her, clouding her spectacles. She laughed again, and removed her spectacles to wipe them on her scarf. Her hands felt clumsy in the knitted gloves because the fingers had been made a little too long.

Then, somehow or other the spectacles slipped through her fingers. She heard a splash and glanced down in dismay. Her spectacles were falling to the bottom of the rocky pool. They lay on the sandy slope, distorted through the shimmering surface, but Miss Frayle could not see them. Panic seized her. She plunged her right hand into the icy water. She could not reach them. Her shoulders quivered in distress. The realisation that she had soaked the sleeve of her mackintosh and her jumper underneath added to her agitation. She tightened her lips to stem the tears that were smarting in her eyes.

'Doctor Morelle always said I'd lose my spectacles some day — and now I have!'

she thought miserably. 'He mustn't know about this.' And again she plunged her arm into the icy water — unsuccessfully. She could not touch the bottom of the pool. She decided she would go back to the hotel as quickly as possible — the Doctor might be still out. Then she would go to her room and ring for the boots and give him half a crown to come down to the beach to retrieve her spectacles. By the time the boots would have returned with the lenses, she would be changed and ready for dinner — and the Doctor need know nothing of the accident. She would he secure from his inevitable sarcasm.

Stumbling slightly, Miss Frayle made her way to the cliff face. Her lack of vision and the almost total darkness made her task difficult. It had been easy enough scrambling down when she could clearly see rocks and undergrowth which she could hold on to — but climbing up again was another problem. All she could see now was the jagged cliff-top above her, and it appeared to be incredibly steep She would have to crawl up, even if it meant ruining her stockings. Gingerly she made her way. She lost her foothold. Breathlessly she paused. 'I can't make it — I can't!' she thought, panic-stricken now. 'I'll be here all night. They'll — they'll find my frozen corpse tomorrow.' Stark terror made her forget the shame of her predicament and she shouted: 'Doctor Morelle! Help! Doctor!' Her voice only sounded like a weak moan against the howling wind. Darkness surrounded her and darkness, too, seemed to creep into her mind. Tripping full length, she lay motionless in a faint.

* * *

Twenty minutes later, Doctor Morelle appeared over the edge of the cliff, armed with a powerful torch and walking stick. He had been told Miss Frayle had been seen cavorting, gazelle-like, to the cliff's edge at dusk. Since darkness had fallen, and she had not yet returned, it did not strain the Doctor's powers of deduction for him to realise that Miss Frayle had inevitably met with some mishap. Deriding her general carelessness and lack of responsibility, he had hurried to her rescue.

When he saw her lying halfway up the path, unconscious, he knelt beside her prostrate form.

'A singularly impulsive young woman,' he told himself, as he prepared to carry her. 'I shall be forced to endure considerable inconvenience — should her exposure result in pectoral congestion. Extremely thoughtless of her!' His feelings were even more exasperated when he trained the torch full on her face, and he discovered that she was without her spectacles.

'Doubtless the cretinous female did not possess the foresight to procure a substitute pair of optical lenses,' he thought testily. 'The routine of my work will be completely disorganised for at least a week!'

He took off his heavy Ulster and put it round her. Sure-footed, he went down the path aided by his torch in search of the spectacles. Ten minutes later he returned, having found and retrieved the spectacles by the simple expediency of hooking them on to the crook of his walking stick dipped into the rocky pool. He wrapped them in his handkerchief and placed them securely in his wallet. Then he carried Miss Frayle back to the hotel where the proprietor's wife placed her in front of a fire, with a blanket round her shoulders, and revived her with hot rum.

She opened her eyes to discover with pleasant surprise she was still alive, and also that her vision was normal. She could clearly see Doctor Morelle gazing at her with a mesmeric stare from the other side of the fireplace. She raised her hands and felt that her spectacles were in their customary position. She giggled light-heartedly.

'I feel — feel — ' she stammered.

'Exactly how do you feel, my *dear* Miss Frayle?' he asked. There was little sympathy in his tone.

'I feel hungry!' she said, and giggled again.

He threw his Le Sphinx into the fire. 'No doubt your peregrinations have given you an appetite for dinner, even though it was it necessary for you to be conveyed home.'

'Oh, Doctor. You rescued me! It was so foolish of me to go down there,' she flustered. 'That was wonderful of you! Thank you and — '

'Your gratitude is redundant,' he snapped. 'My motive in recovering you was completely personal. It so happens I shall have full need of your meagre talents during the next week.'

'Anyway it was very brave of you!' she goggled at him. Then she gave a little laugh. 'When I fainted I had a nightmare. I dreamed that I'd lost my spectacles. Wasn't it lucky that I didn't? You would have had to rescue those, too, Doctor?'

She gazed into the fire, and so she did not see his expression of sardonic and secret amusement.

At dinner, the proprietor himself carried in the roast. Jake Tregarth was a big, bluff Cornishman, genial and anxious to please his winter guests because business was slack in the off-season. He hoped Doctor Morelle might recommend the hotel to some of his medical colleagues. The appetising meal and the double rum that Miss Frayle had consumed soon revived her spirits, despite the fact that the Doctor was morosely taciturn throughout the meal.

When they were rounding off dinner with coffee, she heard a telephone ring in the next room. By force of habit she rose to answer it, realised her foolishness, and sat down again. She caught the Doctor's mocking gaze, and blushed. Jake Tregarth was now answering the 'phone, and although she could not distinguish what he was saying, his tone seem agitated. He appeared through the door a second later.

'Sorry, Doctor and Miss,' he apologised, 'I oughter have knocked. I'm a bit upset. They've just telephoned that there's been an accident. It sounds serious.'

'Have you not informed the local general practitioner?'

'That wouldn't be no good. Old Doctor Tressider be a good chap, but he cures everyone's ills 'cept his own. He's sick in bed and is the only doctor hereabouts.'

'There is no other medical assistance in

the immediate vicinity.'

'That's how it be.'

'Very well!' Doctor Morelle stubbed out his cigarette. 'Tregarth, kindly bring my automobile from the garage — and Miss Frayle, with all expediency, procure my medical instruments, coat, hat, gloves, and stick.'

'Thank you. That be a great help. Doctor — ' Tregarth murmured gratefully.

With Tregarth sitting in the front, directing the way, the car sped through the twisting lanes. Wind howled eerily and rain seemed to be threatening. A storm was blowing up from the sea.

'The accident sounded serious,' Jake Tregarth was saying, 'though I hope it isn't. It's Mr. Penruth, one of an old family. Been in these parts for years. Lived at Armada Farm for nigh on five hundred years — the family have.'

'Armada!' Miss Frayle echoed. 'What a strange name for a farm.'

'Ah well, it be like this, Miss,' Tregarth said, turning to speak over his shoulder. Miss Frayle was huddled in the back of the car. 'The Farm 'tis not far from the sea, and in olden times they do say — '

'Doubtless the Spanish Armada was sighted from there,' broke in the Doctor quickly, as though to cut short some lengthy legend that appeared to be imminent. 'Or some such trivial story.'

'No, 'tis not trivial,' the other protested, and his heavy features looked serious in the flickering light of a match which he held to his pipe. ''Tis a very, very gruesome tale.'

'Indeed?' Doctor Morelle stifled a yawn. 'What is it? Miss Frayle would no doubt be interested to hear!'

'Well the Penruths have lived at the farm for generations, as I said. And 'twas a Penruth gave shelter to a Spanish sailor who was washed ashore from the wrecked Armada. Then — so the story goes — this Penruth murdered him for a jewelled cross he wore.'

'How perfectly horrible!' Miss Frayle exclaimed with a shiver.

'Somewhat inhospitable of him, surely?' commented the Doctor.

'Ah, 'twas murder!' repeated Tregarth.

'Penruth strangled him with the chain of the very cross that he stole from the sailor. And since that terrible day a curse has been laid on every Penruth first son that he'll meet with a violent end. Ah, and always just before his death, the ghost of the Spanish sailor is said to appear at the farm.'

'And — and has the curse come true?' Miss Frayle quavered.

'That it has,' nodded Tregarth portentously. ' 'Tis a funny thing, but folk do say no head of the family has died peaceable-like in his bed. Mr. Penruth — the one who's had the accident, well he be a first son. He come under the curse, you see, Miss, and mark my words, I reckon as — '

'Is our destination in the vicinity at this moment?' the Doctor interrupted as the lane dwindled into a cart track.

'Begging your pardon, we're almost there. This road be awful bad, but you'll be seeing the old farm in no time.'

As he spoke the storm broke and the rain lashed down on the car. The headlights were reflected back in their eyes as they turned through an open gate and past a group of tumbledown outhouses. The old farm itself, badly neglected, was a little to the right, and someone was making an effort to guide them by swinging a storm lantern a few yards ahead of the radiator.

Miss Frayle caught at Tregarth's shoulder. 'Mr. Tregarth, did — did you say the ghost carried a storm lantern?'

Tregarth gave a hearty comforting laugh. 'No, Miss. Now don't you be upsetting yourself about my story, true though it is.'

Doctor Morelle perceived that the dim figure with the storm lantern had halted and was swinging the light beckoningly towards a door.

'The residence possesses a distinctly haunted appearance, I must admit,' he commented, and gently braked the car. 'What do you say, Miss Frayle?'

'It — it is rather gloomy.'

'Me — I wouldn't go into that house for a million pounds,' Jake Tregarth muttered. 'I'll wait here in the car for you.'

'Very well. Come, Miss Frayle.' The

Doctor shone his torch on her. 'And kindly refrain — if you can — from looking like a startled hen!' He opened the door and clambered out. 'Let us announce our arrival.'

He strode through the rain and mud to the door where the figure with the lantern was waiting. They saw a gaunt woman of about fifty with iron grey hair and staring eyes. Her face twitched in some nervous spasm, and she peered malevolently as she shone the lantern, directly in their faces.

'Kindly deflect that illumination from my eyes!' the Doctor snapped.

Begrudgingly the woman obeyed him.

'Thank you,' he went on icily. 'I am Doctor Morelle. Mr. Penruth is expecting us.'

The woman remained motionless, except for the twitching of her features. She did not reply.

'Hm. Ill-trained servant!' the Doctor murmured under his breath.

'Perhaps she's foreign and doesn't understand,' suggested Miss Frayle, helpfully, moving to his side.

The Doctor said to the woman: 'Might we enter?' There was no response. 'I said, might we enter?'

Silently the woman stood back from the doorway.

'She's beckoning us to go in, Doctor,' Miss Frayle whispered in awed tones.

'Is the creature dumb?'

'Doctor, she is! She's pointing to her lips and shaking her head.'

'But she's not deaf apparently,' the Doctor hazarded. At that moment there were heavy footsteps across an uncovered floor, and a man's voice shouted:

'All right, Hannah, I'm coming!'

Through the pale lamplight, they saw a powerfully built man, below middle-age, with a ruddy healthy complexion, and jet-dark hair.

He stepped to the light and clasped the Doctor's hand. 'This is most kind of you,' he exclaimed in a pleasant modulated voice. 'I'm John Penruth.'

'I am Doctor Morelle.' The Doctor inclined his head: 'My assistant, Miss Frayle.'

John Penruth turned to the old woman.

'You may go, Hannah,' he said kindly, and added in a low voice to the Doctor: 'She's dumb, I'm afraid. Result of a shock some years ago. I hope it didn't alarm you.'

'Oh no — not at all,' said Miss Frayle untruthfully. 'Poor creature!'

'And now,' the Doctor said directly, 'perhaps you will kindly conduct me to the sick-room. I have not yet been informed of the nature of the accident.'

John Penruth glanced down at the floor. He spoke in a reverent, hushed tone:

'I — I very much regret that you've made your journey for nothing,' he murmured softly. 'My uncle is dead.'

Miss Frayle gave a gasp of sympathy. 'Oh, how — ?'

'He died a little while after I'd telephoned.'

'I see.'

'His skull must have been badly fractured,' explained John Penruth.

'How did his unfortunate demise occur?' asked the Doctor, applying the flame of his lighter to the inevitable Le Sphinx.

John Penruth closed the front door and then turned to Doctor Morelle and Miss Frayle. There were pained shadows in his grey eyes.

'Uncle fell down the stairs,' he announced, his voice breaking slightly in grief. 'He was a heavy man and he must have struck the lower step with the back of his head.'

'A regrettable accident indeed,' the Doctor murmured, exhaling a cloud of blue smoke.

The other shook his head weightily. 'It wasn't an accident,' he said slowly.

'No?'

'No! My uncle was murdered!'

'Murdered?' Miss Frayle echoed the word in a strangled gasp.

'He was murdered by the Spanish sailor,' Penruth continued. 'Uncle was the first son, you see.' He looked searchingly at the Doctor. 'Perhaps you don't know of the curse of the Penruths?'

Doctor Morelle stifled a yawn with difficulty. 'As it happens I am acquainted with the legend.'

'Legend?' Penruth gave a short, bitter

laugh. 'I tell you it's no legend.'

'You mean the ghost actually killed your uncle?' stammered Miss Frayle.

'I do.' Penruth nodded seriously. 'Either the shock of seeing it caused him to stumble and fall, or the ghost actually threw him.'

The Doctor laughed sardonically. He examined the tip of his cigarette attentively. 'Come, you are asking me to believe a superstitious farrago which has no scientific basis?'

'You must believe it, Doctor,' Penruth insisted. He shot a glance towards the wide uncarpeted staircase. 'I tell you I found Uncle at the foot of the stairs. He was moaning about the Spanish sailor and the curse. He — he said that, after leaving me downstairs, he heard footsteps along the passage. He saw a figure illuminated in the darkness. The figure brushed against him and peered in his face.'

'I can't bear this!' Miss Frayle shrilled in panic, which a second later gave place to curiosity. 'What happened then?'

'Then — why then he lapsed into

unconsciousness, before he could tell me any more.'

'Did you not see anything untoward yourself?'

'No, Doctor, I can't say that I did.'

The Doctor strode across the hall. 'May I be permitted to examine the deceased?' he asked.

Penruth led the way down a narrow passage where an oil lamp, suspended from the ceiling, threw flickering shadows as the wind howled through the cracks in the ill-fitting doors and windows.

'Hannah and I carried him into the morning-room — just through here,' Penruth directed, and pushed open a squeaking door. 'Mind your heads. You'll have to duck.'

A thin blue dust cloth covered the corpse, and quite clearly Miss Frayle could see the outline — the bulge of the forehead and nose, the arms folded across his chest.

'I can't bear to look — ' she burst out, and, gasping in fright, she stood close to Doctor Morelle.

He looked at her disapprovingly out of

98

the corners of his eyes.

'Kindly diminish the volume of your respiration!' he snapped. 'I find it distracting.'

'I've got to breathe,' she protested.

'I fail to perceive any reason why,' he retorted. 'Your presence is more than usually a hindrance. Kindly be of some assistance, and uncover the corpse.'

'Uncover the c-c-corpse! I — I couldn't,' she stammered. 'I — I — faint at the sight of blood.'

'Then pray face that wall, and in order not to cause me further inconvenience, attempt to attain an equable frame of mind by directing your thoughts to pleasant matters.'

He moved over to the body and carefully removed the cloth. Gently he turned the head on one side. He inspected a deep wound at the base of the head, where the skull was obviously fractured, and the blood had congealed darkly on the grey hair. He covered the corpse again.

'Fracture of the cranium,' he pronounced impassively. 'There will inevitably have to be a coroner's inquest, and it would appear as though — '

The Doctor broke off quickly as a terror-stricken woman's scream burst upon them. The three of them turned expectantly to the door. Again the scream rang out — echoing through the old farm. Above their heads came the hurried, panic-stricken scurry of a woman's footsteps.

Penruth moved to the door and paused. He glanced at Miss Frayle and Doctor Morelle in turn.

'Good heavens, what's that?' Penruth asked with what appeared to be unfeigned surprise.

'Presumably a woman's scream.'

The running footsteps stopped, and a shrill voice was shouting:

'Help! I can't get away. I'm on the stairs! It's after me — it's — '

'Who is that hysterical female?' the Doctor asked as he crossed to the door.

'I don't know. There's no one here except us,' Penruth said in agitated mystification, 'and Hannah, of course, and she's dumb!'

They followed Doctor Morelle down the passage into the hall, A dark-clad figure was swaying down the staircase.

'It's Hannah!' Miss Frayle gasped.

'Upstairs! The ghost! Upstairs!' the woman was screeching.

The Doctor moved swiftly up the stairs and supporting her bony shoulders, half carried the hysterical creature down.

'The shock would appear to have restored her speech,' he pronounced.

Penruth, poised on the foot of the staircase, peered fixedly upwards into the darkness.

'Quick, Doctor!' he gasped. 'I'm going to lay that ghost if it's the last thing I do!'

Hannah moaned agonisingly and pitifully clung to Miss Frayle.

'Take care of the woman,' the Doctor ordered her crisply, 'unless you prefer to accompany us?'

'No — no,' she flustered, 'I'll — I'll look after Hannah.'

The woman threw her arms round Miss Frayle, almost stifling her with the pressure of her grasp. A strange smile spread suddenly over the woman's gaunt features. It seemed as though she had forgotten about the ghost, and was marvelling at the return of her own speech.

'Forty years . . . not been able to speak! Now I've got so much to say — !' she babbled.

Penruth was frenziedly hunting in a drawer.

'Just a minute, Doctor,' he was saying over his shoulder. 'There's a revolver somewhere here. We can't take any chance with the Spanish sailor. When I find that ghost, I'm going to shoot it!'

'Do you not mean shoot through it?' the Doctor asked enigmatically.

Penruth raced ahead of him up the stairs, the barrel cocked and the safety-catch clicked back. Miss Frayle, the old woman clinging to her and babbling, tried to see what was happening.

'Follow me — hurry! Hurry!' Penruth exclaimed. He and Doctor Morelle had now reached the top of the stairs. 'Hannah must have seen it on this landing . . . ' He broke off, his voice hoarse with trepidation. 'Doctor, Doctor

— I've just realised!'

'What is it?' the Doctor asked sharply, training his torch into the darkness of the corridor at the top of the stairs.

'I've just realised,' repeated Penruth slowly. '*I* am now the first son of this generation of Penruths. If — if I don't lay that ghost, it'll — it'll kill me. Stay close!'

Penruth suddenly grasped the Doctor's arm.

'It's over there. Look!'

'I do not perceive anything.'

'By that door — in the corner.'

At the end of the long corridor they saw a tall figure in an old-fashioned costume. It was dressed as a sailor of olden times. The figure moved forward and raised its face and round its throat was a blood-red circle.

'Good God! It's the Spanish ghost!' Penruth exclaimed.

The Doctor walked forward steadily to the figure.

'Who are you?' he demanded, in a resonant voice. 'Answer me!'

'Stay where you are! Don't go any nearer,' Penruth cautioned. 'I warn you

— as you value your life!'

'Silence! The apparition is attempting to speak.'

The figure was whispering something; the whispering grew louder. It began to speak slowly:

'A Penruth slew me for my cross, sacred to me ... So henceforth all who bear that name, Penruth, to a violent end shall come ... And the tortures of the Inquisition damn their souls ... '

Penruth pressed forward, raising his revolver steadily.

'I'm going to shoot!' he declared. 'Stand back, Doctor.'

There was the flash and the crack of the revolver.

'It's gone ... it's vanished!'

'So I perceive,' murmured Doctor Morelle.

'Disappeared just like that!' Penruth snapped his fingers. 'Come downstairs, I need a drink.' As they emerged into the lamplight again, he turned to the Doctor with a look of triumph. 'Well, not much of a legend about it, is there?' he commented. 'You saw what happened with your own eyes.'

'A most interesting phenomenon,' Doctor Morelle tapped a Le Sphinx on his thin gold cigarette case.

'Even your scientific mind will have to admit there are more things in heaven and earth than are dreamed of in our philosophy,' Penruth continued. 'I mean, I fired at point-blank range.'

Miss Frayle ran up to them, having extricated herself from the clutches of Hannah, who was now gazing into the fire, muttering disjointedly to herself.

'Are you all right, Doctor? I heard a shot. Has — has the ghost gone?'

'The answer to both your almost incoherent questions, my dear Miss Frayle, is in the affirmative. As for the apparition, it apparently entertained a high view of Mr. Penruth's marksmanship and evidently preferred to disintegrate of its own accord.'

Penruth fumbled in a pocket for a pipe. 'Is Hannah all right?' he asked, glancing over to the huddled figure in the chimney corner.

'She's quite all right,' Miss Frayle

nodded. 'She rather exhausted herself by trying to talk too much. She can hardly believe she's got her voice back.'

'I couldn't believe it either when I heard her,' Penruth observed.

The Doctor drew at his cigarette.

'Doubtless her speech will now be perfectly normal. It is not at all an unusual case.' He turned to Penruth with a bland smile. 'And now, if you will kindly indicate the whereabouts of the telephone I will communicate with the police — merely a routine matter.'

'The telephone's over there by the door.'

'Thank you.' He turned his back full on Penruth and, with long raking strides, made his way across the hall.

'I can't think what good the police'll do,' Penruth called after him. 'One can't expect them to arrest a ghost!'

'Precisely, Mr. Penruth,' speaking over his shoulder as he still continued walking. 'That would be too much to ask of them.'

Penruth started after him.

'You mean, Doctor, that — '

'I mean,' Doctor Morelle replied coldly,

'that a murder has been committed. That an arrest is imminent, and logically one can't expect a ghost to stand trial — '

'Look out, Doctor!' It was Miss Frayle who gave the warning cry. She had seen Penruth pull the revolver from his pocket and raise it menacingly at the Doctor's turned back.

'Doctor! He's going to shoot — '

Penruth's face was twisted into a mask of baffled rage. 'Stay away from that telephone — or I'll shoot. I'm warning you. I'm desperate,' he shouted. 'One more murder won't — '

Doctor Morelle refused to turn round. Miss Frayle marvelled at his coolness. He merely continued walking.

'I'm going to count three and then I'll let you have it — in the back,' shouted Penruth. 'One — two — '

Silently the Doctor strode forward; Miss Frayle could see his motive now. His walking stick was leaning on a table where the telephone stood, just a few yards away. Would he make it in time? Would Penruth shoot him in the back? Or would —

'Three!'

Doctor Morelle grasped his stick casually, and wheeled round to face the threatening Penruth.

'If you do fire that revolver,' he murmured, 'I am confident it will do no more than cause a disagreeable explosion. It is obviously loaded with a blank cartridge, otherwise you would have also killed your accomplice who portrayed the role of the apparition with such polished histrionic ability. As a contrast to the seemingly fearsome weapon, which is now trembling in your grasp, this apparently harmless walking stick that I hold quite firmly, is an exceptionally deadly weapon. Pray observe.'

He quickly unscrewed the hand of the stick and revealed his celebrated sword-stick.

'If you wish to avoid the somewhat nauseating experience of transfixion, I would advise you to remain still,' he continued, and added testily: 'Miss Frayle, do telephone the police with expediency. I am being submitted to a draught from this ill-fitting door.'

★ ★ ★

An hour later, Miss Frayle sat next to Doctor Morelle beside the fire in their comfortable hotel, sipping hot cocoa. Outside the storm thundered at its height.

'I can't think for the life of me,' she pondered, 'how you realised the crime was committed by a human agency. After all you did write once that there was some scientific reason to believe that poltergeists could do physical injury.'

He yawned sleepily. 'No doubt Penruth had also read that statement of mine, and considered that my evidence on those lines at the inquest would have carried a great deal of weight in securing a verdict favourable to him. Actually Penruth was a singularly unskilful psychologist. Like so many people who are educated above their intelligence, he made the mistake of underrating the mentality of others — '

She opened her mouth to say something; he held up a silencing hand.

'It is to myself I refer — not you, my dear Miss Frayle. To underrate your intelligence would be an impossibility. Throughout the day you have been alternately in a state of coma or hysteria.'

'It has been rather a hectic day for me, Doctor,' she excused herself. She leaned forward eagerly. 'But do solve the mystery! You do so love keeping me in suspense.'

Doctor Morelle judicially placed the tips of his fingers together and looked fixedly at the ceiling as he said:

'The murder of Penruth's uncle — he had been struck down by a blow on the head — was ingeniously and elaborately schemed by Penruth himself, aided by an accomplice whom he smuggled into the house. It was the accomplice, however, who during the impersonation of the apparition revealed the plot. The ghost purported to be that of a Spanish sailor of the Armada — yet he spoke in faultless English — a singularly unconvincing achievement! The shot fired by Penruth was, as I deduced, a blank cartridge, intended to heighten the illusion. The servant, Hannah, was not in the secret and really believed it to be a ghost, the shock giving her back her power of speech . . . '

Miss Frayle smiled brightly. 'It's an ill wind that blows nobody any good, isn't it, Doctor?'

'Quite.'

She warmed her hands against the blaze. The moaning wind outside seemed to make the dimly-lit room all the more comfortable.

'I must say,' she said emphatically, 'I was rather suspicious of that ghost myself. I've never believed in spooks since that case at Sevenmeads — when there was supposed to be an apparition haunting the churchyard.' She gave a satisfied smile as he nodded encouragingly. 'I mean to say, Doctor, ghosts — if they do exist — do not have any substance, so why should one be frightened of them? Besides, there must be some ghosts who are friendly and want to help people. They must feel very hurt when they are going to do a good turn to someone and that person runs off in fright — '

He had been listening most intently, nodding in a manner that made her feel that she was voicing some very logical piece of ratiocination.

'What you say is most interesting, my dear Miss Frayle,' he said in a hushed voice. 'Sssh!' His voice dropped to a whisper, and his profile looked portentously saturnine in the firelight. 'Look, the door!' The urgency in his voice was electric. '*It's slowly opening!*'

With an involuntary reflex movement, Miss Frayle bounded to her feet, projecting her spectacles to the tip of her nose.

'But — but who could be there?' she stammered.

He answered slowly: 'I — don't — know . . .'

She clung to the mantlepiece. In a strained, stifled voice, she said:

'Who's there?' She glanced at the Doctor. 'There's nobody.' Panic seized her. 'Oh, Doctor! It's opening wider — who can be coming in?'

He laughed sardonically.

'Merely a puff of that ill-wind you were mentioning blowing in from the hall,' he chuckled hollowly.

She sighed in relief.

'And did you not also mention that you no longer believed in spooks, my dear Miss Frayle?'

'Doctor — how could you — when you know my nerves are — ' she protested in a frenzy of incoherence.

'Kindly affix your spectacles more securely,' he bade. 'Otherwise they may be precipitated and it would then be incumbent on me to rescue them again.'

'Did you say again, Doctor?' she gasped.

'That was the word I employed,' he murmured. 'Who do you imagine rescued your spectacles this evening? One of those amiable apparitions to which you just referred? Come, come Miss Frayle, where's your sense of logic?' He patted her shoulder. 'Now, attempt to procure a restful night's repose.' He walked out of the room. As he was halfway up the stairs, she heard him adding: 'We have some intense research ahead of us, and it will cause me considerable inconvenience should you be suffering through anxiety neurosis due to deficiency of slumber. Goodnight, Miss Frayle . . . '

4

The Case of the Gap in the Curtain

Miss Frayle peered into the darkness, clutched her coat round her throat and wished she dared take Doctor Morelle's arm.

'What a night! Black as ink! And cold too!' she pronounced, with a little shudder. 'Clock striking somewhere. What's the time, Doctor?'

'Half past ten o'clock,' he responded, glancing at the luminous dial that slowed against his wrist.

'Half past ten!' breathed Miss Frayle. She yawned luxuriantly. 'Been a long day today, and I'm tired.'

'Yes Miss Frayle, I, too, feel somewhat somnolent — ' His voice also dwindled off into a yawn.

An hour previously he had been relaxing by the fire, in his silk dressing gown and slippers, preparatory to having an early night. Then that bane of every medical man's relaxation had issued its shrill warning: the telephone rang. It was an urgent call from a patient who lived in northwest London. The Doctor had been compelled to don his outdoor clothes and shoes and, with Miss Frayle carrying the necessary medical equipment, had proceeded by taxi on his mercy errand. He had left the patient sleeping peacefully after inducing somnolence by means of his hypnoscope — a fascinating instrument that consisted of a small light set in a small disc. When held twelve inches in front of and twelve inches above the patient's vision, it induced a strain on the optical muscles, which caused tiredness and a desire for sleep.

Miss Frayle had sat in the bedroom, while he performed this simple hypnosis. His soothing words to the patient had induced a feeling of utter tiredness in Miss Frayle, and it was only with a tremendous effort of will that she managed not to fall into a deep sleep herself. She kept on telling herself that the Doctor would have to carry her home if she fell into a cataleptic coma.

'Relax more,' Doctor Morelle had intoned softly to his patient. 'Just go to sleep, but remember that you are not really asleep, and will hear all that I say to you. As you sleep more deeply you will hear only what I say, and you will cease to hear anyone else speak. Gradually you forget everything, forget everything — everything. Your thoughts are vanishing . . . vanishing . . . '

Miss Frayle's head had nodded dreamily, and if the Doctor had not changed his mode of suggestion to counteract the patient's acute anxiety neurosis, she herself would indeed have fallen soundly asleep. She remembered with a shudder how the Doctor had once told her that sometimes the hypnotist himself became hypnotised instead of the patient. He had instanced a Viennese professor who had been performing this strange science upon a homicidal maniac in a lunatic asylum, and the professor himself had become hypnotised by the staring-eyed patient, and had gone into a trance while the maniac demanded the keys, and had escaped after carefully locking the comatose hypnotist in the padded cell.

As Miss Frayle walked along the dark street beside the Doctor now she shivered. It would indeed have been bizarre, she thought, if both of them had lapsed into a coma, and the poor patient had been compelled to spend a sleepless night watching over them!

Fortunately, such a contingency had not arisen, though the treatment had left both her and the Doctor in a very sleepy condition indeed.

'Where are we now?' she asked wearily.

'In the vicinity of St. John's Wood Road I should imagine.'

She yawned again. 'It's so dark you can't see a hand before your face. Not that I want to see a hand!' she added quickly.

Doctor Morelle was peering round him. 'We ought to procure a hackney vehicle soon — '

He was interrupted by a sudden sharp explosion.

Miss Frayle started. 'Goodness! What's that?' she gulped.

He stopped walking. 'It might have been the hackney vehicle I mentioned having a tyre-burst,' he said with a sardonic chuckle. Then added more grimly: 'Or more probably it was a revolver shot!'

Miss Frayle made an oddly expressive sound — composed of a nervous squeak, a martyred groan and a weary sigh. 'Oh, don't say that, Doctor. Just when I feel so tired. Why do these things always have to happen to us?'

He was turning his head, striving to recapture the direction whence the shot had sounded.

'It appeared to come from the other end of this drive, as if from a house.' Suddenly he turned and began to walk, with long raking strides, through two heavy wrought iron gates. The moon drifted from behind the clouds at that moment, and they saw a wide, winding drive, which was bordered with tall elms. Rapidly the Doctor disappeared down the drive, fully awake and alert now. Miss Frayle trotted mechanically behind him, still yawning.

They reached a corner, and the concrete drive gave way to pebbles. They gazed ahead in the moonlight and both stood still in amazement. Logically they had expected a large. Georgian residence to meet their gaze at the end of such an impressive drive. Instead they saw a diminutive, modernly-constructed bungalow, partly built of timber, and with the moon shining to the right of tiny chimneys above the slanting red tiles.

'It's almost like a doll's house,' Miss Frayle exclaimed in open-eyed wonderment. 'Whoever would imagine there was such a place in London?'

The faint moonlight then faded again, leaving them in total darkness.

'No doubt the family who reside here inherited the land and the manor which was once evidently situated here,' the Doctor deduced practically. 'They would find the domestic problem too acute, and the upkeep too heavy, due to the death duties. They would then have the manor dismantled and in its place they erected this more utilitarian residence.'

'Of course that would be it. I'd never

have thought of it — '

She broke off as she heard heavy footsteps crunching over the ground.

'There's someone coming along the path,' she whispered loudly. Next second she heard an agitated male voice shouting:

'Who's that — ? Who is it?'

A dark form lumbered up to them. Miss Frayle could see only the white blur of a heavy pale face.

'I am Doctor Morelle,' the Doctor pronounced. 'This is my assistant, Miss Frayle. We thought we heard a revolver shot. I wondered if perhaps I might be of assistance.'

The man in the darkness paused breathlessly. Then he said in a terse grim tone: 'Something has happened, I'm afraid. I — I was just on my way to the 'phone-box.'

The Doctor stood directly in front of the man, as he moved to continue down the drive.

'What exactly is the nature of the occurrence, pray?' he queried blandly, his finely cut features appearing more than usually saturnine in the flickering illumination of his lighter as he ignited an inevitable Le Sphinx.

'It's a friend of mine — the man who lives there. He's — '

'Yes?'

The stranger broke off with a convulsive gulp. 'He's committed suicide!'

'How dreadful!' Miss Frayle gulped nervously.

'Why did you not utilise the telephone from the residence?' the Doctor asked calculatingly.

'I tried to — I couldn't get in. The door's locked, and the housekeeper must be out.'

'What is the name of the man who has committed *felo de se*?'

'Alan Russell.'

'And your name?'

'I'm Robert Bell. I live near here. I was visiting.'

'If you have not gained entrance to the house, how have you ascertained your friend is dead?'

Bell spoke quickly. 'I managed to look through a gap in the curtain of the study

— it's the other side of the house, and he'd fallen across his desk. I called him, but he never moved.'

'Oh, poor man!' exclaimed Miss Frayle sympathetically. 'What an awful shock for you!'

Bell was mopping his forehead with a handkerchief. 'Yes, I don't mind telling you, it's shaken me quite a lot.'

'Perhaps he isn't really dead,' Miss Frayle said with tremulous optimism. 'Perhaps he was just injured and is unconscious. Shall we hurry, Doctor?'

She turned and found she was speaking to the empty darkness. The Doctor was already ten paces away, making for the door of the bungalow. She ran after him, Bell following her, and she apprehensively caught on to the Doctor's unyielding arm.

'I'm going to hang on to you like grim death,' she said anxiously, and added with a superstitious squeak: 'Oh, I oughtn't to have said that!'

Doctor Morelle stood on the step and pounded the doorknocker resonantly.

'I'm afraid it's no good,' Bell observed.

'We'll have to break in.'

He stopped knocking, and Miss Frayle strained her ears attentively. 'Someone's coming!' she observed.

It was not her imagination this time. Slippered feet moved across a stone floor, and a slit of light shone through the bottom of the door.

'The housekeeper must have been in all the time!' Bell declared in an amazed tone.

'Unless it's your friend, alive after all!' declared Miss Frayle optimistically.

The group stood tensed as they heard a key grating in a rusty lock. The door opened a few inches and a severe feminine voice demanded: 'Who's there?'

Bell countered with another question: 'Where have you been, Miss Denham?' He spoke loudly, indicating that the housekeeper was slightly deaf.

'Oh, it's you, Mr. Bell. It's my night off. I — er — got back earlier than I anticipated. I hope you haven't been waiting long?'

'*When* did you return?' Doctor Morelle asked sharply.

'Er — a few moments ago, sir,' replied the housekeeper. 'I came in by the back way and had just taken off my coat when I heard you. Come in, sir.' She nodded vaguely to Doctor Morelle and Miss Frayle. 'And you, sir — and you, miss.'

They entered. Although the lights were on in the hall the housekeeper was holding high a lighted candle in a long brass holder. As she closed the door, the guttering flame blew out. She looked at the group critically. She was a little woman, with twinkling eyes strangely set in a face that looked like crinkled parchment. Her dark clothes were of the fashion of about twenty years ago.

'Mr. Russell will be expecting you all, I suppose,' she nodded in a bird-like manner.

Miss Frayle started visibly, and felt a wave of sympathy for the woman. 'What's she mean?' she gasped. 'Doesn't she know — ?'

Bell touched the woman's shoulder comfortingly.

'Aren't you aware, Miss Denham, that Mr. Russell is — er — well indisposed?'

'Indisposed fiddlesticks!' the woman disparaged. 'There's nothing much amiss with him when he does as I say. He's been taking his cod liver oil regularly, has Mr. Russell, and changes his shoes when they get wet!'

The Doctor turned to Bell with his eyebrows raised quizzically.

'Exactly what age is Mr. Russell?' he asked.

'Two years younger than I am.' The other's voice dropped so that Miss Denham would not hear. 'Miss Denham was his nurse years ago. She used to live here when it was a mansion. She's never really believed that he's grown up.'

'Poor thing!' murmured Miss Frayle, blinking through her spectacles sympathetically.

'Doubtless it would be more circumspect not to inform her until we ascertain the nature of the tragedy.'

'What are you whispering about now?' Miss Denham asked snapping her lips in an exasperated manner. 'I won't have it. It's late enough as it is to call on Mr. Russell.'

Bell appeared to be controlling, with some difficulty, the grief that he felt for his dead friend, for the sake of the old nurse. He smiled at her affectionately, and put an arm round her shoulder.

'Now don't be cross,' he humoured her.

'No Mr. Bell, you won't get round me with your smarmy manner!'

She began to walk along a passage that obviously led to Russell's study. Miss Frayle, watching her, fluttered her hands in apprehension. Somehow she must be prevented from entering the room where Russell lay dead. The sudden shock of seeing her beloved charge lying there shot might have serious consequences on the aged woman. Miss Frayle ran after her and caught her arm. She tried hard to stifle the eerie feeling created by this old nurse who lived so much in the past, still regarding her charges as children.

'We've come a long way to see Mr. Russell,' she said, looking pleadingly at her.

Miss Denham tightened her lips, eyed Miss Frayle crossly, and then smiled, relenting. 'Oh, you all know how to twist Old Nurse round your little fingers. Very well, dear, you shall see him.' She tapped on the study door, and then with a nod to them turned and moved in the direction of the kitchen.

Miss Frayle gave a sigh of relief. She glanced towards Doctor Morelle who was watching the disappearing figure with narrowed eyes.

'Interesting case,' he observed, 'Retrogressive mentality!' Then he turned to Bell sharply. 'Perhaps you will conduct us into the room of the demised.'

'Yes, Doctor, this way.' He paused for a moment outside the green painted door, then stretched a hand to the handle, and then withdrew it. The Doctor, noticing the man's distressed hesitancy, moved forward and flung open the door. The room was dark. He stepped inside and felt along the wall for the light switch, clicking it on. They stood in a group in the doorway, blinking in the light, and gazing round the room.

'Oh, look!' squeaked Miss Frayle, backing into the corridor again. 'How perfectly horrible!'

Despite the fact that she had seen many corpses — victims of murders, suicides and accidents — Miss Frayle had never failed to register distress and horror. Her wide eyes saw a large desk in the middle of the room, and a man slumped over it, blood from an ugly revolver wound staining his fair hair.

'Hm . . . life is extinct,' the Doctor diagnosed, reasoning aloud. 'The shot could have been self-inflicted. Yes, the revolver would have logically fallen on the carpet near his foot. And yet — '

The qualification of his hypothesis was interrupted, because at that moment Miss Denham appeared at the door with the supper refreshments on a silver tray. She stood in the doorway, transfixed by the scene. Her lips twitched spasmodically as though she was stricken dumb; then she gave a piercing scream and dropped the tray with a clatter. Miss Frayle ran to her side, her arms outstretched, expecting the old soul to collapse in a heavy faint.

But Miss Denham did not faint. She pulled herself up tensely, so that strangely she seemed to gain quite two inches in height. Her eyes became glassy, expressionless, as though shock had induced stupefaction. Slowly she walked to the group round the dead man. She gazed down at the inert figure, stretched a long thin hand and straightened the collar of the deceased's jacket.

She moved round in a circle like an automaton until she faced Doctor Morelle fully. Then she shot out a pointing finger accusingly.

'You did it!' she screamed: 'You're bad! Bad!'

The Doctor hid his astonishment admirably. It was the first time he had ever been accused of murder. Rather was he usually in the role of the accuser.

'I ought to take a stick to you,' Miss Denham raved as she threshed her arms madly. 'You've caused Mr. Russell harm! Oh, poor, poor man!'

'Pray calm yourself,' Doctor Morelle said insistently. 'We all realise the shock you must feel — '

'Don't you talk to me, you wicked one!' The old nurse fumbled with a locket on her bosom. She unfastened it, held it tightly, and suddenly plunged the sharp pin at the Doctor's face, making downward movements in an effort to tear the skin. He sidestepped and caught her wrist, extracting the locket from her grasp with his other hand.

With firm gentleness he led her to a chair. Her hysteria of violence now seemed to have expended itself. The old nurse moaned helplessly and sank into the chair, looking ahead of her with blank eyes.

Irritably, the Doctor turned to Miss Frayle who met his gaze blinkingly.

'Pray do not stand there in the posture of a startled hen,' he snapped. 'Adjust your spectacles and administer to Miss Denham without delay.'

'Y — Yes.'

Doctor Morelle shot a keen look at Bell, who was trying shakily to light his briar pipe. Then he extracted a handkerchief from his pocket and picked up the revolver with it.

'One cartridge has been utilised,' he pronounced. 'Hm . . . the weapon is still loaded. A service revolver I see.'

Bell nodded numbly. 'That's right. It belongs to Russell. It's the revolver he had in the last war — '

'There's a note on the desk,' Miss Frayle prompted futilely.

'Kindly refrain from stating the obvious, Miss Frayle,' the Doctor retorted as he leaned over the desk. He picked up the note with his handkerchief. Bell moved to his side and, glancing over his shoulder, read the note:-

''Can't go on without you. This is the best way out for us both. I die with your lovely face before me. Goodbye. Alan'.'

Miss Frayle blinked at the Doctor. 'He's referring to the photograph on the desk, that one in the silver frame,' she exclaimed, 'Oh, isn't she lovely?'

'She has a certain photogenic pulchritude.'

The photograph was, in fact, that of an attractive woman, apparently in the middle thirties.

'He must have shot himself looking at her photograph,' theorised Miss Frayle. 'How dreadful!'

The Doctor clicked his tongue impatiently. He turned over the revolver in his hand.

Bell gulped, pushed his pipe into a pocket, and gazed at the Doctor with a puzzled frown.

'He was deeply in love with her,' he exclaimed. 'He told me he was unhappy because she said she couldn't marry him.' His voice broke. 'But I never thought he'd do this. It's terrible. Terrible!'

Doctor Morelle made no reply. He carried the suicide note across to Miss Denham, and held it before her eyes.

'Kindly peruse this note carefully,' he instructed softly, and added in explanation: 'I am only striving to be of assistance.'

Miss Denham turned her eyes hopelessly to the writing on the note.

'Can you state with certainty that this is Mr. Russell's calligraphy?'

'It's his writing,' the old nurse replied in a hollow voice. 'I ought to know, I taught him to write.' She nodded absently. 'Yes, that's the way he made his e's and everything.' She paused, pressing her hands against the edges of the chair in an effort to rise. Exhausted, she sank down again. 'But he couldn't have killed himself,' she protested shrilly. 'He couldn't. He had no reason. She was fond of him.' She clasped her hands frenziedly. 'They might have had some silly quarrel. I don't know — ' Her frail body swayed, and she moaned agonisingly.

'And you still declare this to be the deceased's handwriting?'

'Yes — yes, I've told you once — '

Bell moved across to the Doctor's side and looked at him fixedly. 'I fear you are stressing Miss Denham unduly,' he said firmly. 'If that isn't Alan's writing, whose else could it be?'

'That is exactly what I am attempting to elucidate,' the Doctor retorted sharply. He stubbed his half-smoked Le Sphinx into an ashtray with a gesture of finality.

'What do you mean, Doctor?' gasped Miss Frayle.

'I wish to infer, my dear Miss Frayle, that this is not the calligraphy of Mr. Russell!'

'What!'

'And that it would not be inappropriate of you, Miss Frayle to telephone Scotland Yard.'

'The police!' shrilled Miss Denham. She rose with amazing agility from her chair and wrested the telephone from Miss Frayle.

'I won't have it,' she protested. 'This is my house now, and I won't have any scandal here — '

Mr. Bell also moved towards the telephone, his lips set grimly.

'She's right, Doctor,' he insisted. He grasped the telephone wire as though he were about to wrench it from its fixing.

'Phone Scotland Yard! I never heard of such a thing.'

The Doctor strode to the middle of the room. He put his right hand into a pocket and withdrew the revolver, which he had picked up from the floor.

'Pray do not interfere with the telephone,' he ordered briskly. 'As you see I am holding the revolver which is still loaded.' He nodded formally to Miss Frayle. 'Proceed.'

'I won't let you do it, I won't!'

screamed Miss Denham.

'Kindly remain where you are.'

Miss Frayle was already dialling. She looked up at the Doctor, blinking behind her spectacles.

'What do I tell them when I get through?'

'Merely say it is a case of homicide!' he retorted, skilfully igniting another Le Sphinx with his free hand. He pointed the revolver at Miss Denham and Bell, and added: 'And that I am holding the perpetrator of the crime at revolver point.'

'Did you say perpetrator or perpetrators — singular or plural?' questioned Miss Frayle, not wishing this time to make any slanderous accusations as she had unwittingly done in a previous case.

'Singular,' he snapped, 'as singular as your apparent lack of skill in sifting relevant details to provide the only possible elucidation.'

He sank into a chair, and prepared calmly to await the arrival of the police.

★　★　★

An hour later, Doctor Morelle and Miss Frayle, both thoroughly exhausted, were returning to the house in Harley Street in a taxi.

'Actually, of course, there were two facts which revealed that Bell had murdered Russell,' he was saying in a tired voice.

'Two!' she echoed, with a slight yawn. 'I didn't even spot one.'

'As might be expected!' he retorted with a thin smile. 'Do you not recall at the outset Bell had stated he had perceived Russell's body through a gap in the curtain? Yet when we entered the study it was in darkness. How then could he possibly have seen the deceased prostrate across the desk? The moon, you may remember, was shining from the other side of the house, and could not possibly have reflected into the room.'

'Wonderful!' Miss Frayle enthused dutifully. 'I don't know how you do it, Doctor.'

He permitted himself a modest smile.

'It was simplicity itself to a person with, if I may say it, my powers of scientific ratiocination, and the ability logically to collate relevant detail. So patent were the clues, that I am often constrained to wonder why it is that other people with normal intelligence cannot also elucidate such problems.'

'You're being too modest!' she said, trying hard to keep awake.

'Perhaps that is the explanation,' he said seriously. Then he turned to her with quick suspicion. 'Miss Frayle, am I correct in assuming that you are being subtly sarcastic at my expense?'

'Oh no — ' she yawned sleepily. 'I'm far too tired for anything like that.' She lay back and half closed her eyes. 'You said there were two clues which gave away the murderer, Doctor. What was the second one?'

'There was the *felo-de-se* note, so-called, which Russell was supposed to have penned. Remember it said: 'Can't go on without you. This is the best way out for us both. I die with your lovely face before me', etcetera — '

'Well?'

He clicked his tongue impatiently.

'Do you not realise, Miss Frayle? How could he have died looking at her photograph in the dark?'

'Of course. Why didn't I think of that?'

'Why, indeed?'

She straightened her spectacles. 'Odd how convinced the old nurse was that it was Mr. Russell's handwriting in the note,' she commented.

'A clever forgery,' he said, 'which established that the crime had been carefully and diabolically premeditated. That note will ensure that Bell receives the extreme penalty.'

'How dreadful! And to think that Bell went as far as to murder Russell because he was in love with the woman himself.'

'Yes, jealousy. That was the sordid motive,' the Doctor agreed. 'Jealousy!' he repeated the word distastefully. 'A very unlovely emotion which can cause mental derangement and which certainly interferes seriously with human glandular secretions.'

Miss Frayle stirred herself in the taxi seat. Her eyelids felt heavy. She strived to keep awake, because she had suddenly thought of something that she wanted to tell the Doctor.

'By the way,' she began, 'I read in tonight's *Evening Standard* that the Lucerne Prize for Psychiatric Research has been awarded to Professor Holtz — '

'Professor Holtz!' he repeated disparagingly. 'How singularly unfitting that he should receive such an honour.' His tone became querulous and raised in indignation. 'He has contributed nothing to psychiatry, save a few ephemeral hypotheses. Professor Holtz indeed! Really, it is quite monstrous!'

In the darkness Miss Frayle placed a hand over her mouth to suppress a chuckle, and a yawn.

'You sound rather out of sorts, Doctor,' she diagnosed sleepily. 'Are your glands working properly?'

'My glands! What cretinous nonsense are you babbling now?' He turned his saturnine features to her sharply. 'Really, Miss Frayle, because I decry the award of honour which holds the serious research in psychiatry to ridicule, are you actually insinuating that I — ?'

He broke off, realising that she had fallen into a heavy slumber. In the flickering light of passing street lamps he regarded her severely. He noticed that her coat had fallen open and the cold night air was blowing on her.

'A singularly uncharitable young woman,' he muttered resignedly, 'and a careless one, too. If she contracted a chill, my work would be seriously disorganised.'

He pulled the coat round her, fastening the top button as she still slept.

5

The Case of the Ventriloquist's Doll

'Kindly hand me that retort, Miss Frayle,' said Doctor Morelle as he bent over some chemicals which he was distilling over a Bunsen burner in his laboratory. 'Also the crucible lid.'

She grasped both the required articles in each hand, and moved across to him. Then, quite suddenly, she caught her breath, her eyes screwing up and her lips quivering. Her shoulders began to shake in an uncontrollable spasm.

'Quick, Doctor,' she managed to gasp. 'Take them! Quickly. Oh!' He jerked round rapidly, eyeing her with baleful displeasure, and relieved her of the retort and the crucible lid. Frenziedly she clapped her hands over her mouth and nose and ran from the laboratory as though she had a sudden premonition it would blow sky-high any moment. She heard the Doctor's sardonic laughter following her as she retreated.

She slammed the laboratory door, and leaned supportively against the door handle. She gasped for breath. Relief came over her features, then puzzlement. Again, she breathed deeply. At last the paroxysm quivered on the brink of its climax.

'A-Ah-A-tis-*SHOO*!' she sneezed violently. She smiled breathlessly. That was a near thing! If she had sneezed when she was holding the chemical apparatus, she would undoubtedly have smashed it. Also, if she had sneezed in the laboratory she would have been the target for a farrago of sarcastic abuse from the Doctor. She sneezed again — it was a refined squeak this time rather than an explosive detonation. With tears in her eyes she laughed to herself. Here she was, sneezing her head off — and there in the laboratory was the Doctor pursuing his research for a final and efficacious remedy for the common cold. There was irony for you!

As though by auto-suggestion, she had

contracted the cold the very day Doctor Morelle had announced his intention of experimenting with the distillation of some new drugs which might prove to be a cure for colds.

'It is singularly inconsiderate of you, my dear Miss Frayle,' he had told her testily, 'to contract a chill while our research is still only at the formative stage. If you had postponed the attack for two weeks you might have been useful at our final experiments.'

'I don't think I'd care to be used as a guinea pig!' she retorted.

'How odd,' he had observed. 'I should have imagined that you would have raised no objections.'

'I think that remark's a little unworthy of you, Doctor,' she had retorted indignantly, but unfortunately had been constrained to rush out of the study to sneeze before he could reply, and so she was never to know whether, for once, she had effectively succeeded in crushing him.

She broke off these speculations when she heard an imperative ring at the front door. She ran to open it. A dark, bulky figure loomed through the doorway and, without even glancing at her, made as if to move past her.

'Whom do you wish to see?'

'Doctor Morelle of course, who else?' The huge man spoke in an authoritative manner. She ran after him, noticing in greater detail his appearance after the first shock of his peremptory entrance, the man would be about fifty, over six feet tall. He was wearing a heavy, dark overcoat with a massive fur collar. A large-brimmed, black hat was on his wide head, and from under the hat she could see red hair curling long down his neck.

'Have you an appointment?' she demanded. The impressive-looking stranger did not even deign to turn his head as he said:

'I do not need an appointment,' and he continued striding along the hall.

'Does the Doctor know you?' she asked anxiously.

'Everybody knows me,' was the terse reply. 'The whole world! The Doctor will be honoured to see me.'

Miss Frayle had by now caught up with him. She was frantically trying to evolve some strategy. Only a few weeks previously she had permitted two gatecrashers in the house at the time when the Doctor was investigating the Wolf Spiders Case. His terse admonitions for her gross carelessness were still fresh in her mind. She tried hard not to be impressed and abashed by this dynamic caller. Desperately, she attempted to classify him. He was either someone very important — or a lunatic! And if he were a person of some importance he ought to know better. Frantically she grasped at the man's arm as he began opening doors in his search for the Doctor. He was already about to fling open the door of the laboratory.

'No — you don't!' she cried. She pushed herself in front of him, and barred his way, stretching her arms across the door. She felt rather like the heroine in a melodramatic film, and she would have said: 'Over my dead body!' if she could have made it sound convincing.

'Stand aside!' he ordered. 'My time is valuable!'

'I won't stand aside!' She felt that she was going to sneeze again. Would — would she then be compelled to release her hold on the door? 'If only you'd make an appointment — '

'Appointment!' The man twisted his lips scornfully. '*I* do not have to make an appointment — I arrive!'

'Yes, so I see, but — ' she squeaked helplessly and she thought: 'If he does see Doctor Morelle, he'll be the only man in the whole world who's a match for him.' The pair of them would be a good team in a contest of bombast, conceit, self-satisfaction and downright rudeness.

'You do not seem to realise who I am!' the man said tersely. 'I am — '

At that moment the laboratory door opened.

'Oh, dear!' gasped Miss Frayle. Doctor Morelle looked over her shoulder at the tall, massive intruder. There was an indignant tightness about his features.

'Whomsoever you may be,' he retorted icily, 'I happen to be Doctor Morelle.'

A condescending smile of welcome came over the other man's features. The

Doctor returned it with a freezing glare. Then he studiously turned away from the man and addressed Miss Frayle.

'What does this disturbance mean?' he demanded.

'I'm sorry, I tried to stop him. But he pushed his way in. He walked right in without a word, started opening doors — '

The man held a silencing hand to Miss Frayle. He bowed gravely to the Doctor, removing his hat with a sweeping gesture.

'I am Voxio,' he declared resonantly. He made the declaration with an air of finality, as though the fact would explain the most eccentric behaviour.

'Voxio!' repeated Doctor Morelle distastefully. 'So far as I am concerned the name might be that of some patent medicine for the alleviation of laryngitis.'

The intruder's dark eyes flashed, but it seemed as though the man's haughtiness dwindled and the corners of his flexible lips drooped. Behind his veneer of bombast, there appeared to be genuine distress. He drew himself up and he

147

seemed to tower over Miss Frayle and the Doctor.

'I am not a medicine, but an artist! Voxio, the Ventriloquist,' he intoned impressively. 'You must listen to me. I am here to beg you to restore to me my little boy.' Suddenly the big man began to sob. His distress and tears seemed almost ludicrous because of the colossal size of the man. 'My little boy has been kidnapped,' he went on dramatically. Then in a down-to-earth tone, he added: 'He's been stolen by some dirty, thieving rat!'

'Oh, you poor man,' burst out Miss Frayle, with her effervescent sympathy which never failed to find expression. 'How worried you must be! No wonder you rushed in here as though you were out of your mind.' She turned to the Doctor, her eyes pleading behind their lenses.

He did not even glance at her. It was as though she had not spoken. With raised eyebrows the Doctor addressed the ventriloquist.

'I presume you are referring to the theft

last night of the effigy with which you give your performance,' he observed enigmatically. 'The occurrence is reported in this morning's *Telegram*.'

The ventriloquist nodded with grief-stricken vigour. He pulled agitatedly at the fur round his collar.

'Yes, yes Doctor. I happened to meet the theatrical correspondent of the paper later. As a personal favour I let him have the — what's the phrase for it? — the exclusive story. I never take the paper myself — too highbrow. What does it say?'

Doctor Morelle reached for that morning's *Telegram*, which lay on a rack near the laboratory door.

'I was reading it only half an hour ago.' He scanned the column, 'This is the item, I believe.'

Voxio took the paper from him and read in trumpet-like tones: ' 'Exclusive to the *Telegram*. After the conclusion of his performance at the Rotunda Music Hall last night, Voxio the Ventriloquist's doll disappeared. It is believed' — '

'Oh, your *doll*,' broke in Miss Frayle. 'I

thought you meant your son had been kidnapped.'

'Doll!' echoed Voxio with vibrant scorn. 'My Joey is more than a doll. He is more human than you, young lady — or your Doctor. He *is* a son to me. Doesn't he work for me, keep me from starving? Doesn't he sleep beside me? Doesn't he — ?' He became incoherent in his expressions of devotion. 'But never mind,' he went on at last, 'you wouldn't understand. What you might understand is that he must be found in time for my show tonight. You must find him, Doctor.'

Doctor Morelle backed into his laboratory, half closing the door.

'Really, Mr. Voxio,' he said definitely, 'I hardly think I can undertake — '

Voxio waved aside his excuse. 'I have heard of you, Doctor,' he stated. 'You are a brilliant investigator.'

Doctor Morelle coughed and half smiled self-effacingly.

'Well I — ' he began.

'Almost as brilliant as I am a ventriloquist,' added Voxio, smiling widely as though he had conferred on the

Doctor the greatest compliment in the world. 'Come, I have a car waiting. We will go to the theatre and there you can pick up the clues. I implore you to find my Joey before tonight. Please, please, Doctor Morelle.'

The Doctor paused ponderously. Finally he nodded his head briskly.

'I will elucidate this mystery for you,' he stated, 'if you will promise to give me a certain undertaking.'

'Anything! Anything!' Voxio repeated, sweeping an arm expansively. 'Money, recommendations, even a free box for the second house on Saturday night! Just name it.'

'Next time you happen to contract a common cold, I would deem it a favour if you would kindly attend my laboratory where I may be afforded the opportunity of administering to you a special drug on which I am now experimenting.'

'Willingly,' Voxio smilingly agreed. 'I'm often getting colds. Have to get over them quickly at my job. Joey and I have to joke about it on the stage.' The ventriloquist, to exemplify his statement, launched into a two-voiced ventriloquial patter: ''How did you get that cold, Joey? — I opened the window — You opened the window? — Yes, I opened the window and in-flew-enza'.' Patiently Voxio waited for the laugh, but as Miss Frayle felt another sneezing spasm coming on she dared not open her lips. The Doctor was not amused. Voxio shrugged his shoulders hopelessly. 'Anyway we have to joke,' he finished. 'I'll stick to my bargain, Doctor, and you can experiment any time you like.'

In the car, Doctor Morelle insisted that Miss Frayle sat in front beside the driver so that she would not fill the atmosphere with microbes. However the sliding window was open, and she could hear Voxio giving Doctor Morelle more details about the disappearance of his doll.

'Of course this tragedy would never have happened if my own dresser had not been away sick,' he was saying.

'Dresser? I fear I am not cognisant — '

'The fellow who looks after my costumes, lays them out and runs errands.'

'In his absence doubtless you are employing a substitute?'

'For this last half of the week. He's nothing but a fool — an idiot!'

Doctor Morelle unwound the window and flung out his Le Sphinx.

'Do you suspect anyone — him, for instance, the substitute — er — dresser?'

'He hasn't the sense!'

'Is he a cretin?'

'I don't know about that. But he's a halfwit.' Voxio stroked his chin thoughtfully. 'Joey might have been stolen by one of my enemies,' he pondered. 'As a successful artist I have plenty — '

'I can understand that,' murmured the Doctor softly.

'That may be it,' declared Voxio, pursuing his train of thought and missing the sarcasm. 'One of my enemies might hope to do a deal with the insurance company. Joey is insured for three thousand pounds.'

'Good Gracious!' exclaimed Miss Frayle involuntarily from the front of the car. 'What a lot of money!'

'A mere bagatelle,' countered Voxio

airily. 'Joey is worth it and more. He is human, I tell you — more human than — ' he looked at Doctor Morelle as he searched for a simile.

'Quite!' The Doctor cut him short. He bent forward to peer out of the taxi window. 'Is this the place of entertainment at which we are drawing up?'

'This is the Old Rotunda. Only a number two house,' Voxio said condescendingly, 'I'm playing it just as a fill-in.' He paid the driver and gallantly armed Miss Frayle onto the pavement. 'The stage door's round this side — next door to the fish and chip shop. Disgraceful locality!'

In a dusty cubbyhole by the red painted stage door, a dour, grey-headed man, shirt-sleeved, and unshaven, gave them no more than a cursory glance. It might have been Miss Frayle's imagination, but she thought that he glowered at Mr. Voxio.

'Any telephone messages?' Voxio asked aggressively.

'Somebody did telephone about something, left their name and message,' the doorkeeper muttered sullenly. 'Dunno what it was all about.' He yawned. 'I've gorn an' forgotten.'

'You should write the message down. This is monstrous,' Voxio stormed. 'I'll report you.'

'I dare say you would like to see me lose me job,' the man muttered under his breath, 'me with a sick wife and two growing kids.' He turned his back on Voxio. 'Stage folk ain't what they were.'

'Silence — impertinent wretch!' Then the ventriloquist turned to the Doctor with a synthetically bland smile, 'Come, Doctor — come, Miss Frayle.' He strode like a king down the dusty, squalid corridor. 'Jealousy! Professional jealousy,' he was observing.

'A great artist has to suffer such indignities from the lower orders.'

Doctor Morelle lit a Le Sphinx, and said:

'I think you would have been better advised to have gone to the police in the first instance.'

Already, it seemed, he was regretting that he had undertaken the investigation.

Voxio clicked his tongue in scorn. 'The police? Dolts! Thick-headed blunderers! No, you are the one who will solve this affair. This way, please. Along here is my dressing room. I have the star one, of course.' He paused as he saw a dark-clad figure disappearing into an office at the end of the corridor.

'Pardon me one moment while I speak to our far from genial manager,' he said, and strode away muttering: 'I really must report that insolent doorman before I forget. Disgraceful!'

'My time is not at your disposal all day!' Doctor Morelle called after him with quick impatience, but Voxio had already entered the manager's office. His indignant, bombastic voice could be heard complaining loudly.

Miss Frayle straightened her spectacles thoughtfully as she waited.

'Did you notice, Doctor, what a nasty look the stage doorkeeper gave him, when we came in?' she asked.

'I fear I cannot blame anyone for regarding him with certain disfavour,' he commented.

'He has an objectionable way with him, hasn't he?'

'So vain, so aggressive. They are two qualities I abhor.'

Miss Frayle sighed and with difficulty refrained from making the obvious comment.

Doctor Morelle exhaled a cloud of smoke. 'He would appear to enjoy delusions of grandeur, almost bordering on paranoia,' he diagnosed. 'Many successful men, I have observed, appear to have almost pathologically inflated egos. Interesting. I wonder if delusions of grandeur help them to success or whether success makes them — '

His psychoanalytical ponderings were interrupted by the return of Voxio.

'The fool of a manager refuses to dismiss the stage doorkeeper,' he announced. 'It's monstrous! Disgraceful!'

Miss Frayle smiled in relief.

Voxio moved towards his dressing room. 'Here we are — in here.' He noticed that the door was ajar. 'Hello, who left the door open?' He glanced inside. 'Albert!' he exclaimed. 'What the

157

devil are you doing here?'

Miss Frayle entering the room saw a pale youth fiddling with some jars of make-up on a long table, which stood underneath a mottled mirror. The youth started and dropped a jar. He stooped to recover it and almost tripped over himself.

'I jest thought I'd come in an' tidy up a bit like, Mr. Voxio,' the youth said in a whining voice.

'But you are supposed to be sick, in bed.'

'I know — but I'm not much of a one for sticking in bed — makes me 'ead ache,' this youth exclaimed. 'Up all last night I was, coughing. Then this morning reads what 'appened in the *Echo*, so I gets out of bed and comes along in case I could 'elp, see?'

He rubbed a grimy hand over his nose.

'I told the new feller you'd engaged, that you wouldn't be wantin' 'im today, seeing as 'ow I've come back, sir, and I can dress you tonight.'

'Very well, Albert. But it's strange — the doorman never said you were here.'

'P'raps 'e didn't notice me come in.'

'He wouldn't — never notices any-thing,' Voxio declared, 'any more than he noticed anyone last night who could have taken Joey.'

'Wasn't it a terrible thing to 'appen, Mr. Voxio?' the youth commiserated. 'When I reads about it in the *Echo*, I thinks to meself, now 'ow will pore Mr. Voxio manage . . . '

'Yes, yes, I can quite imagine how you felt!' The other cut him short. He turned to the Doctor and pointed to a brown case that lay on one end of the table. 'This is the case in which Joey is kept. When, after leaving the theatre, I had the intuition all was not well and returned here, the case was as you see it now.'

Doctor Morelle walked across to the case and examined it closely. Miss Frayle peered over his shoulder. He said:

'The locks, both of which are of intricate pattern, have not been forced. Well, Miss Frayle, what would you deduce from that significant fact?'

'Someone must have used a key,' she declared, with what she thought was commendable promptness.

'Precisely.' He permitted himself a faintly derisive smile 'For once you have found the truth in the obvious — you are improving.'

'Thank you, Doctor!'

He inspected some lettering at the base of the container.

'Observe too,' he said softly, 'that the receptacle is of foreign manufacture.'

'It was specially made for me in Rio de Janeiro,' declared Voxio removing his wide-brimmed hat and propelling it skilfully on to a hook. 'Wasn't my south American tour an enormous success Albert? The crowds! Colossal!'

'Yes, Mr. Voxio,' murmured Albert dutifully. 'You was a sensation. They'd never seen anyfink like you afore.'

'True! True!' The ventriloquist struck an attitude. 'Voxio the Great — Voxio, the *Unique*. It might be an idea for a billing Make a note of it, Albert.'

'Very good, Mr. Voxio.'

'Your assistant accompanied you on your world tour, I gather?'

'Yes, everywhere,' the other replied with

a sweep of his arm. 'Let's see — how many years have you been with me, Albert?'

'It's going on for three years. You'd promised arter the first year to give me a rise, but I 'aven't — '

'Tush! This is no time and place to broach such a trivial matter, my lad.'

Albert was about to make some protest, but was interrupted by a tap at the door. A shock-headed man of about thirty put his head round and appeared embarrassed when he saw so many people in the dressing room.

'Oh! Good morning, Mr. Voxio — I just looked in. I'll come back later,' he declared in a thin Cockney voice.

'Come in now. Close the door, you dolt!' ordered Voxio. 'Miss Frayle has a cold.' In a stage whisper, Voxio hissed at Doctor Morelle: 'This is the other dresser, the fool!'

'I see.'

' 'Appened to be passing the theatre, I did, and — I thought I'd look in to see 'ow Albert felt, 'im not having been well. I thought 'e might need an 'and,' the man twisted his cap in his hands, 'and I 'oped I might see you too, Mr. Voxio.'

'And why?'

'Well, begging your pardon, sir, and excuse me mentioning it in front of this lady and gentleman, but I — I er — '

'Go on, you fool!'

'I thought you might want to settle up with me for the two days I've been working for you, seeing as 'ow you won't be needing me now Albert's back an' all.'

'The matter will be attended to.'

'Oh, thanks . . . Sorry about your trouble, sir, about Joey I mean. You could 'ave knocked me down with a fevver when I 'eard . . . '

Doctor Morelle eyed the substitute dresser piercingly.

'I understood you were the last to leave the dressing room last night? In accordance with instructions you locked the door after you?'

'S'right, sir,' the man nodded. 'Left the key on me way out. The doll — I mean Joey — was safe and sound in his box then — Mr. Voxio'd tucked him up 'isself.'

'I would not let a clumsy idiot like you touch him.'

'No, Mr. Voxio,' the man said meekly enough. Then, with a bright smile he added: 'But look 'ere, instead of messing everyone about, why don't you call the perlice? They'd soon — '

'Shut up!' snapped the ventriloquist. 'When I want your advice I'll ask for it. Now get out.'

'I think in point of fact you might take his advice,' Doctor Morelle said softly.

'What — what? Do you mean to say that you cannot — '

'As I am not in a position to take the culprit into custody, the presence of the proper authorities would be advisable,' the Doctor.

'Culprit? You mean you know the thief? You know who's taken my Joey?'

'Precisely!' Doctor Morelle swiftly walked to the door and closed it. 'In fact I'd go further and state that the thief is now in this room.'

'In this room? Here?'

'I speak plainly, do I not?'

' 'Ere, 'oo are you accusing?' gasped

the Cockney substitute dresser. 'I could 'ave the law on you for that.'

'So far, I have not specified the thief — ' the Doctor retorted calmly.

'Well, if it ain't Albert, ye're accusing me, and I won't 'ave it. Jest 'cause I'm new — and I 'elps Mr. Voxio out of his fix, Albert being ill — '

'Calm yourself, you fool!' Voxio shouted. He glanced in turn at the two dressers. One of them was guilty. Which? Albert was sullen, looking as though he'd begin to whine at any moment. The new man was defiant, indignant.

'Well, who is it, Doctor?' Voxio asked, clenching his hands tightly.

'The young man who bears the name of — Albert,' the Doctor declared.

Albert rushed forward, the corners of his mouth working frenziedly. His thin hands caught at Voxio's coat pleadingly.

'I didn't mean to keep it,' he babbled. 'I'll bring it back to you . . . I'll find Joey again. I sold it to a man in a cafe. I've got the money 'ere in me pocket. I'll find the man again and . . . '

The veins showed on Voxio's forehead.

With one large hand he grasped the back of Albert's coat.

'Wretch. Ungrateful swine!' he shrieked. He raised an arm and crashed it down full in Albert's face. With the other hand he gave him a resounding slap across his mouth.

'I'll thrash you to death,' he cried. He was like a madman. 'You fiend, treating my Joey like that I'll — I'll — '

He grasped the swaying youth, and fixed his large hands round his thin neck, pressing against his windpipe with his wide thumb.

'Do something, Doctor Morelle!' cried Miss Frayle. 'He'll murder him. He'll — he'll . . . ' Her shoulders shook in a wild paroxysm. 'A-A-Ah-tis-*Shoo*!' she sneezed.

'Desist, Voxio!' the Doctor ordered.

'I'll kill him!'

Doctor Morelle approached the big man from the rear, grasped his left elbow, and twisted quickly, catching the other in a ju-jitsu lock. Albert broke free and fell against the wall, sobbing.

'To preserve you from a murder

charge,' the Doctor said levelly, 'I think it would be advisable if I escorted Albert to the police station myself.'

'I'll come quietly,' Albert sobbed breathlessly. 'Get me away from him! Don't let him come near me. He's — he's a — cruel swine, 'e is. Everyone 'ates 'im. Everyone . . . I 'ope 'e never gets Joey back, I 'ope. I won't tell where — now — '

Babbling incoherently, Albert followed Doctor Morelle and Miss Frayle from the room, while the ventriloquist sank on to a broken-down settee, and watched them with stupefied eyes. It seemed as though he knew he would never see his beloved doll again and the blow stunned him.

★ ★ ★

Later in his study Doctor Morelle lit a Le Sphinx, and took a deep draw at it.

'Strange how a man should lavish every modicum of his consideration and devotion on a doll,' he was reflecting, 'and yet have none for his fellow creatures.'

Miss Frayle straightened the papers on her desk.

'It's Albert I feel sorry for,' she declared. 'Do you think they'll send him to prison, Doctor?'

'I think not.' He tapped the ash from his cigarette. 'I shall make it my business to speak for him at the police court proceedings. Since the creature was not engaged in crime previously, he will be indubitably bound over on probation. I will make a point of using my influence with the probation officer to find him more harmonious employment.'

'Why — why, Doctor Morelle! That is most awfully kind of you,' Miss Frayle uttered in astonishment.

He regarded her quizzically.

'Am I to assume by the surprise in your tone, my dear Miss Frayle that you consider acts of kindness are foreign to my nature?'

'No, Doctor Morelle. Oh, no!' she exclaimed. 'It was just that — ' she became confused, and decided it would be safer to change the subject quickly. 'I think you were awfully clever over that case. How could you possibly deduce Albert had stolen the doll?'

He sank into a chair and gazed ceilingwards. 'It was quite obvious to me he was the thief,' he said calmly, 'as he admitted, on the way to the police station, he had contrived to obtain duplicate keys of the effigy's case and the dressing room. Providing himself with an alibi by his pretence of illness, he had slipped into the theatre that night and removed the effigy. The stage doorkeeper, used to seeing him at the theatre, had not noticed him on the occasion in question — an easily compre-hended fact and one which induced me firstly to believe the thief might be someone connected with the music-hall.'

'But how did he give himself away?'

'He revealed himself as the culprit when he stated he had read of the theft in his newspaper, the *Echo*, while in bed that morning. Voxio had mentioned it only to the correspondent of the — as he described it — highbrow *Telegram* which printed the affair as an *exclusive* report. In other words, the knowledge of the occurrence was not in the possession of the *Echo* or any other newspaper. Thus, the young man, in seeking to ward off any suspicion and ingratiate himself with his employer by arriving at the theatre, did, in fact, incriminate himself.'

Miss Frayle nodded understandingly.

'And, of course, Doctor, it was most unlikely that he ever read the *Telegram*,' she observed.

'Quite — a journal of somewhat erudite composition and intellectual aspect.'

'Or, 'just a stuffy old paper' would be a concise and apt description, eh, Doctor Morelle?' she suggested mischievously.

'My dear Miss Frayle!' Irritably he stubbed out his cigarette. 'When I am desirous of tuition in colloquial English, I will advise you. Furthermore, I really must request you to — to — '

He broke off quickly. His eyes suddenly went glassy. He appeared to be panting for breath. He stood up, took a quick step forward and paused spasmodically.

'What is it, Doctor?' she asked anxiously. 'Don't you feel well? Are you ill? Oh, what is it?'

Doctor Morelle opened his mouth. His

eyes closed. His limbs jerked and he moved quickly to the window, flinging it open and thrusting out his head and shoulders. His answer to her question burst on her ears with an explosive report.

'A-Ah-Ah-tis-*SHOO*!'

6

The Case of the Solicitor's Legacy

Though Doctor Morelle considered himself unique in most respects, he had to admit he was human enough in his susceptibility to that ubiquitous leveller, the common cold. Furthermore, in accordance with the precepts of his profession, he accepted the axiom that once the germ responsible has established itself, the cold must take its course. So, at the first intimation of a chill Doctor Morelle, in this respect at any rate, practiced what he preached, and invariably took to his bed, armed with a bottle of medicine of his own dispensing, and proceeded to make Miss Frayle a partner in his suffering.

Directed by his instructions issued from his sickbed, she ran innumerable errands, placated disappointed patients who wished to see the Doctor, cancelled engagements, kept up the fire in his room and reminded him when it was time to take his medicine. In spite of all her burdens, however, she made her characteristically conscientious efforts to carry them out and at the same time cheer up the patient.

Even when he sardonically informed her she must be under the influence of a 'Florence Nightingale' fixation, she persevered with her bright smile and perhaps somewhat irritating 'bedside manner'. Occasionally, when one of his rebuffs was particularly bitter, her eyes behind her spectacles would blink with mortification. But pretty soon she was addressing him once more in that indulgent tone usually reserved for a very spoilt child.

She stood outside his bedroom door one morning, rather dreading the coming day. He had now passed beyond the hoarse stage of his cold, when, his voice lacking its familiar biting qualities, he had been forced to refrain from unleashing his sarcastic observations upon her efforts to play the ministering angel.

Miss Frayle was bringing him the morning papers. These, she hoped, would keep him occupied for half-an-hour at least, before he began demanding her attention to deal with the day's routine of errands and the usual variety of problems. This morning she had an added problem on her mind. There was a piece of news in the papers that she felt might upset him. She was in a quandary as to whether she should bring it to his notice. As she went into his room, she decided since it would be impossible to keep the papers from him, she must think of some way in which to break the news to him gently. Steeling herself for the coming ordeal she put on a bright and cheerful smile and advanced towards the bed.

'Miss Frayle, will you please remove that fatuous grin from your features whenever you enter the room,' came the acid voice from the pillows. Its familiar incisive timbre was there, she noted with dismay. 'And would you be good enough to close the door — ' he added maliciously: ' — from the other side preferably? You may not be aware of the fact, but I am confined to bed with a chill, and if my recovery is to be expedited, I must avoid all draughts.'

She closed the door and returned to the bedside. The Doctor was lying muffled in a thick bed-jacket over his pyjamas. A half-empty box of Le Sphinx cigarettes at his elbow and one between his lips indicated he had not curtailed his smoking as part of his self-imposed treatment.

'You sound much better this morning,' she said cheerfully.

He blew his nose aggressively, and stared at her through a cloud of cigarette-smoke.

'Judging by your highly complacent tone, Miss Frayle,' he rasped. 'I should imagine you have something unpleasant to announce!'

He shuddered as she smiled brightly again and became busily attentive.

'Oh, dear! your eiderdown has slipped off,' she chided him, as she replaced it. 'Did you notice that new after-chill tonic advertised in the papers this morning?' she rattled on. 'They say it's just the thing to put you on your feet after a cold.'

'I am quite capable of standing on my feet when the time is opportune without any assistance of the nature you suggest!' he snapped irritably. 'Not that I have had an opportunity of perusing the morning journals, which you have placed so thoughtfully out of my reach.'

She handed them to him.

'I will start the day by reading the obituary column of *The Times*,' he decided thoughtfully. 'And reassure myself that I am fortunate enough to be in the land of the living!'

He was folding the paper when Miss Frayle interposed nervously:

'Er — Doctor — I think — that is — I ought to tell you — '

He fixed her with a mordant glare.

'As I divined, Miss Frayle! No doubt you wish to confess to some negligence? You have possibly blown up my laboratory? Doubtless from your point of view a mere trifling mishap — '

'Oh no, no Doctor,' she interrupted in extreme agitation. 'It's — it's — something in the paper!'

He eyed her shrewdly, then turned to the paper he held.

'What sensational headline devised by the editor for the gullible public has caught your over-developed imagination?' he murmured.

'It isn't anything like that. It's — it's about Mr. Gordon.'

'You mean James Horace Gordon?'

'Yes.'

He suddenly snapped: '*Will* you be good enough to close that window? How often must I impress upon you the need for me to avoid draughts?'

She sighed and closed the window, which was open half-an-inch. 'You mustn't be a molly-coddle, you know,' she reproved him. 'After all, you've only got a chill, and you've got me to look after you. Not like poor Mr. Gordon.'

'That is a debatable statement!'

'Mr. Gordon is — well, he's dead!'

The Doctor's eyebrows lifted the merest fraction.

'Dead?' he murmured.

'According to the papers,' she went on, 'he was gassed!'

'Are you inferring it was a case of *felo de se?*'

'Suicide, it says in the paper.'

Doctor Morelle sighed, but made no comment. With a thoughtful expression he began to search his newspaper. He found the report, which read:

'In the early hours of this morning, James Horace Gordon, solicitor, of Quadrant Chambers, Field's Inn, was found dead in a gas-filled bedroom. The police were summoned by his man-servant, William Goodchild, who said that his employer had lately been subject to severe fits of depression . . . '

Doctor Morelle paused in his reading to give a gigantic sneeze. He blew his nose and leaned back on his pillows, his eyes closed, his face wearing an abstracted look.

He was recalling to mind the last occasion on which he had seen James Horace Gordon. He had enjoyed a very pleasant dinner with the old man at his bachelor chambers, followed by a lengthy discussion on various aspects of forensic medicine.

They had met some years ago. The Doctor had given evidence in a case as a result of which Gordon's clients had received a stiff sentence. Out of this unpromising first encounter had developed a friendship between them based on a professional admiration for each other. They did not meet very often, for both were very busy men, respecting each other's immersion in his vocation.

But the Doctor knew he had only to telephone the little old solicitor if he required any assistance in any legal matter. In his turn Doctor Morelle was always ready to help Gordon.

He had once commented on the fact that the old man enjoyed such robust health that he never seemed to be in need of medical aid.

'Moderation! That's the secret, Doctor!' the other had smiled. 'I know my limits, and I never exceed 'em. Still, if ever I do, I promise you the first opportunity of diagnosing the trouble.' He had paused and added: 'I'll tell you something that will amuse you. Though I've spent most of my career in advising people to make wills, disentangling and contesting wills and administering 'em, I never made a will of my own till last week!' He had chuckled reminiscently. 'Something seemed to tell me I'd pass the three score and ten mark. All our family have been long-livers, so I waited until I was seventy, and now I've done the job.'

Then he had given the Doctor a long look, his eyes twinkling beneath his shaggy eyebrows. He had said:

'By the way, I've named you as an executor.' The Doctor had expressed his appreciation of the honour, and had observed:

'I sincerely hope, however, I shall not be called upon to act in my executorial capacity for some years to come.'

Doctor Morelle opened his eyes and regarded Miss Frayle, who was busying herself making the room tidy. He sat up in bed.

'I should be more grateful, Miss Frayle, if you would refrain from disturbing any further particles of dust, which I have repeatedly advised you is a major irritant, and instead put me into telephonic

179

communication with Scotland Yard!'

'Scotland Yard?'

'I wish to speak to Detective-Inspector Hood immediately.'

'But you know you oughtn't to have any excitement,' protested Miss Frayle. 'It will only send up your temperature.'

'*I* am experiencing no sensation of increase in my pulse rate,' he snapped.

'You're supposed to lie quiet and take some of this medicine,' she insisted.

'A moment ago you were accusing me of indulging in self-pity,' he accused her.

' 'Phoning Scotland Yard indeed!' cried Miss Frayle, with a show of indignation. 'Before we know where we are we'll be rushing off and getting mixed up with bodies — and then you'll catch pneumonia and be a body yourself!' She added by way of an afterthought: 'And I shall lose my job!'

'Will you please telephone Inspector Hood?' snapped the Doctor through clenched teeth, glaring at her.

'Listen to you!' she challenged him, her voice rising to a squeak. 'Why, you're looking flushed already!'

He was rapidly losing the remains of his patience. 'It is you who are unable to control yourself!' he exclaimed, choking with annoyance. 'I am not in the least excited!'

She eyed him uncertainly.

'Will you make that call!' he demanded, 'or do I have to jump out of bed and strangle you with the telephone cord?'

He looked as if he were about to spring out of bed there and then and put his threat into operation. Miss Frayle positively dived for the telephone, on the bedside table, and began dialling. As a result of his ill-tempered agitation, the Doctor lapsed into a fit of coughing. Miss Frayle interrupted dialling to pour out his medicine. He was just gulping it down with an expression of profound distaste and she had started to dial the number again when the front-door bell rang.

Still coughing and choking, Doctor Morelle waved her to go and answer it. She returned a few minutes later with a little frown and regarded him with a look of trepidation.

'It's a Mr. Goodchild,' she said. 'He

— he says he must see you — it's most important.'

'Goodchild?' His eyebrows shot up.

Then his face took on an expression of interest. 'Gordon's manservant,' he said half to himself. 'Bring him up immediately.'

'I told him you couldn't possibly see anyone,' she insinuated.

His gaze was baleful.

'Bring him up!' he snapped, and another paroxysm of coughing shook him. Apprehensively Miss Frayle retreated to the door.

'Very well, Doctor, but do remember you mustn't excite yourself!'

'Will you go, woman!'

She vanished.

A moment later a thin-faced man sidled apologetically into the room. He wore a shabby raincoat over a morning suit, and carried a trim black bowler hat. Miss Frayle hovered in the background and closed the door for the newcomer as he moved towards the Doctor.

'Good morning, Doctor Morelle, I'm sorry to have to trouble you like this, but it's important. Most important.'

'Sit down,' said the Doctor, eyeing him with his penetrative gaze. 'I presume you have come to acquaint me with the facts relating to Mr. Gordon's unfortunate demise?'

Goodchild nodded sadly.

'Tell me exactly how the tragedy occurred?'

'There isn't really very much to tell, sir,' the man muttered, sinking on to a chair Miss Frayle had placed for him, his bowler hat perched on his knee.

'Mr. Gordon appeared to be in fair health, except that he had seemed somewhat depressed these last few days. Unusual for him, as you know. However, he was apparently no worse when I said 'Goodnight' to him last night. Soon after one o'clock this morning, I woke up suddenly. I imagined I could smell gas. I put on my dressing gown and went on to the landing. The smell was stronger there, and I traced it to Mr. Gordon's room. I knocked, but there was no reply. I went in. He was lying face downwards on the rug in front of the gas-fire. The tap was on, but the fire wasn't burning. He was dead, I could tell that at once. I telephoned the police, and they seem to think it is suicide.'

Doctor Morelle stared at the man over his cigarette.

'And what opinion have you formed?'

'I — I don't know, Doctor.'

'I am under the impression that you have not paid me this visit merely for the purpose of acquainting me with what you have?'

Goodchild shook his head. Fumbling in his inside coat pocket, he produced an envelope.

'I found this on a table in his bedroom. Addressed to you. I didn't know whether I should have given it to the police, but I thought I'd come to you first. In case it's anything private.'

Miss Frayle saw the Doctor frown as, taking the envelope and opening it, he read:

'Dear Doctor Morelle,
I deeply regret this step I am about to take, but feel I have lived beyond my

allotted span. You will find my estate in good order, but I wish to make a small addition to my will. I want you to pay the sum of five hundred pounds to my head clerk, Jonathan Taylor, and the same amount to my manservant, William Goodchild, in recognition of their services to me during my lifetime. Thank you, and goodbye,

James Horace Gordon.'

Thoughtfully refolding the letter and replacing it in the envelope, he said:

'Mr. Gordon gave you no hint of the contents of this letter?'

'No, Doctor,' replied Goodchild. 'He never discussed his private affairs with me.'

'Quite so. I am glad you brought this communication direct to me. It may have an important bearing upon the circumstances surrounding your employer's demise.'

Goodchild nodded. He sighed heavily.

'Yes . . . Oh, what a shocking affair. Poor Mr. Gordon. No man could have wished for a more considerate employer.'

He twisted his bowler hat round in his fingers, looked a little uncomfortable, then stood up.

'Well — ' he muttered uncertainly — 'If there's nothing else, Doctor? The young lady said I wasn't to stay long — '

'It may be desirable to get in touch with you again. No doubt you will remain at your present address for the time being?'

'Until after the funeral, Doctor.'

'Miss Frayle will show you out.'

'Thank you, Miss. Good morning, Doctor . . . '

When Miss Frayle re-entered the room a few minutes later, she was astonished to find the Doctor sitting up in bed, the bedclothes swathed round him and speaking into the telephone.

'Is that Detective-Inspector Hood?' he was saying.

'Good morning, Doctor Morelle,' came the cheerful reply.

'As a small return for the invaluable assistance I have given you on numerous cases, perhaps you would be good enough to acquaint me with one or two details

186

concerning the late Mr. James Horace Gordon?'

'You mean the solicitor who committed suicide early this morning?'

'You are satisfied it *is* a case of *felo de se*?'

'Oh yes,' came Hood's confident voice over the wire. 'We're just conducting a routine check-up. As a matter of fact, I'm in charge of the case.'

'That may be fortuitous!' remarked Doctor Morelle. 'Inasmuch as I may be able to render you some further trifling assistance in its connection. Who is conducting the *post mortem*?'

'Oh, Sir Richard'll be doing it.'

'Convey my compliments to him and advise him that I should be particularly interested in the results of the blood test. Furthermore, I should be interested to know whether or no he discovers any traces of bruises. Also the position of the blood in the lungs.'

'What the devil are you driving at, Doctor?' the detective queried in a puzzled tone.

'Finally,' went on Doctor Morelle

coolly, 'would you inform me if you have found the deceased's will?'

'Yes, we've got that. I have it here on my desk.'

'I desire to peruse it. You will no doubt observe that I am an executor.'

'Yes, I can read English, too!' the Detective-Inspector came back at him good humouredly.

'It is a facility for *reading between the lines* which *I* find more profitable!' was the swift, sardonic retort. 'Kindly bring the document along immediately after the *post-mortem* has been performed. Doubtless you will let me have the results of that simultaneously?'

'All right,' agreed the other. 'But you talk as if it wasn't a plain case of suicide,' he grumbled, mystified.

Doctor Morelle merely gave a sardonic chuckle and replaced the receiver. He turned to see Miss Frayle standing at his side with another glass of medicine.

'Really, Doctor,' she reproved him, 'you will catch your death if you go on like this.'

'On the contrary, I feel very much

better!' he snapped. He took a sip from the glass and choked. 'Ah! What a vile concoction!'

'You mixed it yourself!' she reminded him sweetly. 'Drink it up, you know it's for your own good.'

With a baleful glance at her he drank it off. There followed several minutes of spluttering, coughing and groaning. When he had finally recovered from the taste of the medicine he sat upright in bed, lit a Le Sphinx, and observed thoughtfully:

'H'm . . . this affair closely resembles the famous mystery of Marie Roget.'

'Who was she?'

'A young female who figured in one of Edgar Allan Poe's tales of ratiocination and detection. Marie Roget was drowned in the Seine, and — '

'But poor old Mr. Gordon wasn't drowned. He was gassed . . . At least — '

He gave a ponderous sigh and shook his head hopelessly.

'If, instead of formulating theories of your own,' he said through his teeth, 'you would allow me to continue my speculative processes without interruption, you would be performing *some* service!'

She subsided and he went on:

'The Marie Roget affair was solved by Auguste Dupin, the fictional detective created by Edgar Allan Poe, simply by perusing the newspaper reports and documents relating to the case — '

'Oh, I see what you mean, now, Doctor!'

He ignored her interruption and proceeded in his characteristically pompous manner:

'Most authorities agree that the tale was founded on fact; that the author based it upon the mystery of a certain Mary Cecilia Rogers who was murdered in New York in 1841. The circumstances surrounding her tragic demise baffled the police authorities and the assassin was never apprehended.'

He paused for a moment as a thought struck him. Then he puffed a cloud of cigarette-smoke ceilingwards, murmuring to himself:

'It would be interesting to obtain access to the newspaper files and documents relating to the Mary Rogers homicide case and, with their guidance, step back into the past and solve the mystery.' He sighed. 'That would be a triumph of deduction! To elucidate a homicide long since perpetrated and left unsolved — '

'I don't see that it would do much good,' objected Miss Frayle. 'Whoever did murder the poor girl must be dead themselves anyway, so why bother?'

He surveyed her pityingly.

'Naturally, my *dear* Miss Frayle,' he said in a silky tone, 'I cannot expect you, with your limited range of intelligence, to appreciate the fascination of such an achievement in the abstract. My preoccupation with criminology has little to do with the human element. The protagonists concerned are merely ciphers; what attracts me to the investigation of crime is the putting into practice of my powers of deduction, my unique aptitude for assembling the facts in their logical and relevant sequence, my — '

'That will be Detective-Inspector Hood,' interrupted Miss Frayle as the front-door bell rang. With a thankful sigh and an expression of joyful release that was not lost on the Doctor, she rushed out quickly to admit the visitor. Doctor Morelle puffed viciously at his cigarette and made a mental note severely to reprimand Miss Frayle at the first opportune moment for her manifest boredom when he was discoursing so enthusiastically upon that most interesting of all topics — himself.

Inspector Hood sat himself by the bedside, and extracted a bulky envelope from the briefcase he was carrying.

'There you are, Doctor, that's the will.' And he passed the document over. Doctor Morelle in turn handed the detective the letter Goodchild had delivered.

'While I peruse the will, you may care to examine this letter consigned to me this morning by the deceased's manservant.'

Miss Frayle sat and watched breathlessly as, for a few minutes, the only sound in the room was the rustling of papers. Then the Doctor looked up.

'Well?'

'Looks fishy to me,' said the other grimly, tapping the letter with a stubby forefinger. 'D'you think they are both in it — this clerk chap as well as the manservant?'

Doctor Morelle shook his head slightly, with a sardonic gleam in his eyes.

'Why not?'

'For the simple reason that in his will, Gordon bequeaths Jonathan Taylor the sum of one *thousand pounds* — Gordon had told me he had mentioned this matter to Taylor and advised him on purchasing a practice of his own in due course — Goodchild, however, was unaware of this fact, and doubtless thought it would avert suspicion from himself if he brought in a second party.'

'He's a deep 'un!' was the Detective-Inspector's comment.

The Doctor took another Le Sphinx and lit it. He went on:

'Unfortunately for himself, he made one serious mistake. He did not realise a meticulous solicitor like Gordon would never have written a letter containing such an injunction, for it has no validity whatsoever. It is virtually impossible for him to have perpetrated such an elementary legal error. He would merely have added a codicil to his will, which was quite accessible in his office safe.'

'I'll pass the letter on to the experts,' said Hood. 'It may not be a forgery, of course. Goodchild may have compelled the old chap to write it, and then murdered him.'

'It is not impossible that Gordon wrote the letter himself under intimidation,' agreed Doctor Morelle, and added: 'Fully conscious that what he was writing was invalid, and confident that I should detect it and from it deduce that foul play had been committed.'

Miss Frayle gave a little gasp of admiration, and the Detective-Inspector looked fully impressed.

'The *post-mortem* proved it was no suicide anyway,' he said. 'Though how the devil you guessed — '

'I never indulge in guesswork,' Doctor Morelle corrected him coldly. 'I arrive at my conclusions by the process of pure reasoning and the application of logic.'

'Well, you were right. Not a trace of gas in the blood. Several bruises were disclosed which might have been caused by violence. Sir Richard's theory is that the poor old chap was smothered with a pillow, and afterwards the body was laid face downwards — but the blood was found to have settled towards the back of the lungs, which would have been impossible if he had died in that position.'

'You say Sir Richard established that several bruises had been inflicted?'

Hood nodded.

'And it seems only a little blood had leaked into 'em, so Gordon must have died very soon after they were inflicted. Another indication he couldn't have inhaled a fatal dose of gas.'

'H'm,' murmured the Doctor with a touch of sarcasm, 'it would appear that a case for culpable homicide is conclusive!'

'And — thanks to you — the identity of the murderer established,' grinned the detective amiably. He rose and produced his pipe. 'Well, I'll be getting along to arrange about a warrant for the arrest of our friend, Goodchild.'

He turned as he moved from the bedside and said:

'Hope you get better quickly. Next time I call, I'll bring you some grapes.'

'I am deeply touched by your solicitude

on my behalf,' came the reply. 'But I fear your generosity would be entirely wasted so far as I personally am concerned.'

'Why, d'you expect to be up and about so soon?'

Doctor Morelle smiled what he hoped was his most wistful smile. 'No,' he sighed, ostentatiously weary. 'Merely that Miss Frayle would devour the grapes while I should be permitted to lie here on my bed of pain unattended and unrefreshed by your kind offering.'

'Oh, Doctor Morelle! How could you — ' she protested. But she was drowned by the detective's laughter. At the door he paused.

'Well,' he said admiringly, 'this is the first time I've ever heard of anyone solving a murder without leaving his bedroom!'

'You should read an article of mine,' murmured Doctor Morelle, 'on Auguste Dupin, the detective character created by Edgar Allan Poe. It appeared in the *London Archive*, Miss Frayle will hand you a copy as you go out.'

And he relaxed on his pillows and closed his eyes.

7

The Case of the Man in the Nightmare

In a lecture room at the Wigmore Hall, London, W.1, a small group of distinguished people craned forward to listen eagerly to the tall, saturnine figure on the platform. His high forehead, his erudite manner and the deliberate dogma of his tone commanded their attention. Sparingly he used gestures, so that when he did stress a point by gesticulation, the emphasis was potently telling.

Doctor Morelle, lecturing on the Bio-Chemical Relationship of Man and Reptile, was making revolutionary revelations to an audience of distinguished scientists, biologists, experts on psycho-neurology and metaphysicians. Scientific history was being made at this moment. New, fierce light was being thrown on the theory of evolution. Everybody listened tensely — with a feeling of marked

197

excitement. Everybody, that is, except the young woman slumped in a comfortable armchair at a corner of the platform. Her spectacles were slipping precariously from her nose. Held laxly between her fingers was a pencil, and in her lap was a notebook; open at a page where shorthand hieroglyphics dwindled off into a faint scrawl. The young woman was not at this moment conscious of what was happening.

Some minutes previously her head had nodded, her eyelids drooped. The warmth of the room, and the steady drone of the Doctor's voice, had induced in her a feeling of intense drowsiness. Her head fell forward, and her subconscious took control.

While all else in the room was keyed tensely to hear the Doctor's revealing words, Miss Frayle slept peacefully on.

Doctor Morelle concluded with a terse and succinct summary of the more salient points of his address. He strode back across the platform, flung himself into a chair, folded his arms, and regarded the gathering with almost ferocious challenge.

There was a tense, electric silence for a few seconds. Then the applause suddenly broke. One man in the front row — a distinguished, bearded surgeon — rose to his feet as he applauded, and, to a man, the rest of the listeners did the same, to demonstrate the signal honour justly accorded to a man of Doctor Morelle's scientific genius. He stood in acknowledgment, and with a synthetically deprecating smile, walked off the platform, to be surrounded by congratulatory groups. His hands were shaken vigorously. He met the admiring gaze of men who were giants of scientific research, and behind his naturally restrained impassiveness was a hint of triumph, indicating that this was indeed one of the biggest moments in his life.

Meanwhile Miss Frayle still slept.

'A revelation, my dear Doctor Morelle!' Professor Brandt was saying enthusiastically. 'In one hour you have revolutionised entire theories of biochemistry. This will have world-wide repercussions.'

'Truly a *tour de force*, Doctor,' another famous man congratulated. 'I trust we shall be able to procure printed copies of this lecture.'

'My address will, of course, be published, Sir William,' the Doctor nodded emphatically.

He lingered to answer questions. The group round him was thinning, as the celebrated audience took its departure. Doctor Morelle himself had reached for his hat and coat and stick. When he was near the door, he slightly averted his head and called out:

'Miss Frayle, we are leaving!'

There was no reply. Testily, he glanced round the room. His narrowed eyes scanned the platform, and opened wide in anger as he saw her slumped down in the chair, her spectacles by this time precipitated to the open notebook on her lap. He strode down the room and on to the small platform. Impulsively he picked the notebook from her lap, and his tongue gave a click of impatience as he saw that she had made only half a page of notes. He reached out a hand to shake her, and then deciding against this course, he carefully took the spectacles from her lap and held them securely. She would leap to her feet like a startled hen when she was awakened — he deduced — and the spectacles would be broken. Since indubitably she did not possess the foresight to procure a substitute pair of lenses his work would be even further disorganised.

'Miss Frayle, murder is about to be committed!'

He snapped the words into her right ear. Immediately she leapt to her feet, her hands flew to her face protectively and she gave a shrill scream.

'Oh, Doctor Morelle!' she cried. 'Help! Help!'

'It is from others you should demand protection — not from me,' he said suavely. 'It is *I* who advocate the homicide, my dear Miss Frayle.'

'Oh, euthanasia!' she murmured in relief, blinking her eyes sleepily.

'Indeed, it would be a mercy killing!' he snapped briskly, 'because you are a singularly useless member of the community.'

She gave a nervous laugh. 'You do love to frighten me, Doctor,' she said. 'Oh, do give me my spectacles. You look so ferocious when I can't see you properly.'

'You will discover that I appear even more fearsome when you affix your astigmatism-corrective lenses,' he retorted sharply. 'Apparently my erudition induces a somnolent condition in you.' He loomed over her. 'Is it of no consequence that my revelations are now lost to posterity?'

'Don't make such a fuss. We'll be able to work it out from your notes.'

His lips tightened impatiently.

'I did not utilise my notes, Miss Frayle,' he declared, 'I spoke extemporaneously.' He grabbed his stick and strode from the platform, snapping over his shoulder: 'Follow me, and do not provoke me farther, otherwise I fear I may lose my self-control.'

Wearily she grabbed her hat and coat and followed him. Through the swing doors that led to Wigmore Street seeped a grey fog. Outside in the November night it was dense. It had spread from the Thames like a thick blanket enveloping the metropolis.

'Oh, it's foggy, isn't it?' Miss Frayle remarked brightly, wishing to divert the Doctor's mind from her recent misdemeanour.

'Your flair for stating the obvious amounts almost to genius! Pray, do not dawdle!'

'Don't you think it would be better if I held on to your coat?' she suggested. 'Then if you happened to walk into anything — '

'You would be preserved from injury! That was your sole object, I presume,' he interjected. 'Signally considerate of you, my dear Miss Frayle!'

'I was thinking you might stun yourself, and if I was stunned, too, you might be lying there for hours with no one to rescue you, and you'd contract pneumonia, and then — well — I'd never forgive myself.'

'Most unconvincing!'

However, he suffered her to do as she suggested, and she trotted behind, dreading that she would kick his heels and so provide further crushing recriminations. Fortuitously, Wigmore Street is but a short distance from the house in Harley Street, although there are several turnings to be negotiated. After they had traversed some distance Miss Frayle piped up anxiously:

'I think we ought to go back, Doctor. I'm sure we've missed the turning.'

He ignored her suggestion, and continued walking. His footsteps slackened slightly as, near a corner, a door suddenly opened and there was a restrictedly diffused quadrangle of light. A figure came running blindly down the steps and collided with the Doctor.

'Excuse me,' a man said excitedly and breathlessly. 'I'm so sorry. I didn't realise the fog was so — '

'It's all right,' replied Miss Frayle readily enough, because she had not been the person who had suffered from the collision.

'I'm dashing to a 'phone,' the man explained in a pleasant, youngish voice. 'Ours is out of order, and I must get a doctor!'

'A doctor — ' she repeated in an attempt to be helpful.

'Yes, yes. Excuse me,' the man flustered. 'I'm so sorry — ' His voice dwindled off as he plunged into the fog. 'Must get a doctor.'

Miss Frayle waited for some response from Doctor Morelle. After a short pause, he cleared his throat.

'Didn't you hear what that man said?' she queried.

'I did, Miss Frayle.'

'Well then, why didn't you tell him you're a — '

He gave a heavy sigh. He turned round on her, so that she almost tripped over his heels.

'Have you not yet learned,' he demanded, 'not to expect the obvious from me?'

'But the poor man was so upset,' she protested. 'Something awful must have happened.'

'Doubtless,' he commented laconically. 'And precisely what that is we will now proceed to ascertain.'

'Where are you going?'

'Into the house, the door of which appears conveniently open,' he retorted. He was already mounting the steps.

'Come, follow me. Let us enter.'

They walked straight into the hall, which in the dim light and the creeping fog appeared to be decorated in a heavily oppressive and rococo style. On all sides, it seemed, stuffed, gaping pikes and swordfish leered at them malevolently. There were antlers and horns and animal skins on the polished floor, so that Miss Frayle had to tread warily to avoid slipping headlong.

'What an eerie place!' she shuddered. 'I can just imagine something terrible happening here. I wonder — wonder what did happen.'

'That, no doubt, we shall soon discover,' he reflected coolly.

Adjacent to a staircase at the end of the hall was a narrow corridor. The door of a room at the end was ajar and a light showed through the opening. Doctor Morelle walked towards it, pushed open the creaking door, and stepped inside. Miss Frayle paused. Whenever her nerves were taut she always had a dread of entering a strange room.

'Is — is it all right, Doctor?' she called

out tremulously. 'Are — are there any bodies?'

She heard him merely click his tongue and she entered the room, her curiosity being stronger than her fear. She glanced round the room, and her eyes widened in astonishment.

'How quaint!' she exclaimed. 'I've never seen anything quite like this before.'

The large room was normally furnished as a kitchen, with this difference: all the furniture was strangely diminutive. Tiny chairs were set against a kitchen table, which stood no higher than two feet from the red-tiled floor. A gas range, sink, refrigerator, and kitchen shelves were also no taller. On a rag-bit rug by the open fire were two small armchairs, and on one was the knitting of a ludicrously diminutive pullover. Strangest of all was a dog kennel, which stood in one corner. It was huge, quite the largest piece of furniture of all, and in front of it was an outsize dog saucer, which contrasted oddly with the tiny plates on the kitchen table,

'What do you make of it all, Doctor?'

Miss Frayle's eyes goggled behind her spectacles.

'It is obvious. There is only one explanation — '

'But I can't understand — ' she puzzled.

'No doubt you soon will.' He lit a Le Sphinx. 'Apparently no one is here. We will investigate elsewhere.'

They returned to the hall again. Miss Frayle glanced around her in wonderment.

'Oh, look at that lion's head up there!' she exclaimed. 'It's frightening — so real.'

'Species *Felis Leo Africanus*,' he classified it.

Miss Frayle stepped back to view it. A sudden chill suffused her whole body. She could distinctly feel a claw touching her shoulder, and against her cheek there brushed a hairy hand!

In a shrill scream she found her voice.

'Doctor! It's a grizzly bear — !'

'Rendered harmless by a skilled taxidermist,' he noted calmly.

'Oh!' She gave a nervous laugh. 'How foolish of me to be frightened. There was nothing to be scared about really — '

She broke off as from the top of the staircase she heard the growling and snarling of some animal. Next second she clung to the Doctor in another paroxysm of panic. A huge Alsatian, its fangs bared, bounded down the staircase and leaped towards her.

'Merely a species of *Canis* — ' the Doctor began.

'Oh, it's a dog! Why didn't you tell me?' This time her sigh of relief was shortlived. The Alsatian leaped from the third step, and, springing up, thudded his front paws against her shoulder. It pushed her over and she lay, paralysed with terror. Quickly the Doctor grasped the dog by the collar, and wrenched it from her.

'He'll bite you,' Miss Frayle cried.

Indeed, the dog now rounded on the Doctor, its teeth bared. Still struggling with the animal, he fearlessly pulled his face close to it. Its fangs opened and then closed as he fixed it with a mesmeric glare.

'Down, and be still . . . '

The dog's growl died to a deep

whimper. Its lithe, tense body relaxed, and slowly it sank to the floor, its great head resting on its paws, and the fiery eyes watching the Doctor. The dog's smooth, grey and brown flank moved steadily as it breathed with rhythmic regularity.

'You've hypnotised it, Doctor!' she whispered in awed tones. She glanced towards the door, at the fog billowing through, and the forbidding grey darkness beyond. 'Let's go, before it becomes dangerous again.'

He answered in an undertone.

'If I avert my eyes from the animal for a single instant, it is liable to attack. We must wait here until the canine becomes cataleptic.'

'How long will that take?'

'Half an hour — possibly even an hour!'

'Oh dear!'

The situation was unnerving — although ludicrous. Here they were in a strange house, with the Doctor glaring fixedly at a ferocious dog — and thus they were likely to remain for thirty minutes at least!

'I wonder what it all means,' she pondered with a shiver. 'That man rushing out for a doctor; the doll's furniture in the kitchen and this mad dog — '

She broke off as she heard soft footsteps at the top of the stairs. She glanced upwards anxiously. At first she thought the approaching figure was a child. Then she saw it was a man less than three feet tall, with a face that would have been childish, if it hadn't been so lined and wizened. But the most bizarre thing was that he was attired in a miniature butler's tailcoat. He bore himself with the conscious dignity of a manservant.

The Doctor slightly averted his head to watch the midget coming down the stairs. The dog stirred uneasily, the whites of his eyes showing.

'Do you require anything?' the midget asked formally, successfully concealing any astonishment he may have felt at discovering two strangers in the house.

'I understand the presence of a doctor is required,' murmured Doctor Morelle.

'You mean you're the doctor?'

211

'I am Doctor Morelle.'

'The young man told us that — that — ' Miss Frayle tried to explain.

'Mr. Travers? Yes, he went out to telephone for one,' the midget observed.

'It was fortuitous his encountering me en route. Now, if you will kindly inform me how I can be of assistance — '

'Be careful!' Miss Frayle warned him. 'The dog!'

The dog had stirred out of his hypnotic helplessness and was growling fiercely. It tensed itself on its haunches about to spring. The midget wheeled round on it.

'Quiet, Demon! Behave yourself, Demon! Good boy.'

The Alsatian ceased its growling, amiably padded to the little figure's side and nuzzled its nose in his hand.

'Demon is unaccustomed to strangers,' the midget explained. 'I am sorry if he alarmed you. I will lock him up in the kitchen.'

He grasped the animal by the collar and led him down the corridor. They made a grotesque picture as the dog meekly allowed itself to be controlled by a human being almost smaller than itself.

'What extraordinary power he has over it,' Miss Frayle exclaimed, as she watched the pair disappear.

When the midget returned, he pointed up the stairs.

'Perhaps you will follow me, please?' he requested formally. 'The — er — body, that is, Colonel Muir is this way.'

'Body!' echoed Miss Frayle. 'Oh dear! This is going to be something awful again!'

The diminutive manservant paused near a door at the top of the stairs.

'I helped Mr. Travers bring him in here,' he declared, and he raised a small hand to his mouth politely as he coughed. He opened the door. 'There, Doctor — ' His alto voice fell to a reverent hush. 'Though I'm afraid he's past aid, poor Colonel Muir . . .'

Doctor Morelle glanced through the open doorway, and turned to Miss Frayle.

'Doubtless you have no desire to — er — view the body.'

'No! Oh, no!' she gasped, and she drew back from the doorway.

'Perhaps, then, you would find Mr. Travers forthwith and deter him from obtaining further medical aid?'

The midget looked up sharply at the Doctor, a puzzled frown on his miniature features.

'But I thought Mr. Travers summoned you here?'

'If you will assist Miss Frayle to find Mr. Travers, she will explain everything to you.'

For a moment the little man hesitated. Then: 'Yes, of course, Doctor.'

Miss Frayle disappeared down the stairs, followed by the midget. Doctor Morelle turned into the room where the dead man lay. Calmly he examined the multiple injuries that had caused Colonel Muir's death. Just as he was completing his examination he heard footsteps and voices on the stairs, and Miss Frayle and the midget returned with the young man whom the latter had referred to as 'Mr. Travers'. She had evidently explained somewhat clumsily the Doctor's presence in the house, because the young man's eyes were blazing indignantly.

'What the devil do you mean entering the house without my permission? When I bumped into you in the fog, I told you I was looking for a doctor, but instead of volunteering your aid, you creep in here behind my back!'

Doctor Morelle calmly surveyed him through a cloud of cigarette-smoke.

'Your haste was such that I had no time to introduce myself. When you disappeared into the fog so suddenly I realised the situation must indeed be urgent, and I entered the house with the object of volunteering my services.'

Travers brushed a frenzied hand through his hair. As he moved towards the light, it could be seen there were bloodstains over his jacket.

'I understand, Doctor,' he nodded, more calmly now. 'Sorry I spoke like that. I'm a bit on edge.'

'Naturally.' Doctor Morelle gesticulated to the body, which lay on a *chaise-longue*. 'Colonel Muir, I assume, met his death by falling from a not inconsiderable height, did he not?'

'He fell from a second storey. The

window leads on to a narrow balcony, edged by a railing. The railing must have given way under the Colonel's weight. It is broken. You can see for yourself if you wish.'

The Doctor closely examined the tip of his Le Sphinx, and asked:

'Were there any witnesses to the — er — accident?'

'Yes — my aunt. She told me she'd seen him fall,' Travers volunteered. He seemed to be labouring under an intensely-felt grief. 'I rushed down and — and I found him on the pavement.'

The Doctor inclined his head towards the midget who stood stiffly and formally by the door. 'And, assisted by your manservant, you carried him in here?'

'Yes — yes. He — he was dead then.'

'His neck was broken. Death must have been instantaneous.'

Miss Frayle shivered violently, and then tremblingly straightened her spectacles.

'What an awful thing to have happened!' she gasped.

Travers sank into a chair, and covered his eyes with his hands.

'Poor Uncle! Oh, poor Uncle!' he murmured brokenly.

'Your aunt actually saw him fall, you say?' queried the Doctor, stubbing out his cigarette.

'Yes.' The other looked up bleakly. 'She's upstairs, in a terrible state, of course.'

Miss Frayle's eyes were round with sympathy. 'Is there anything I could do?' she asked.

'No, no — thank you.'

Doctor Morelle said:

'I will go up to her in a moment.'

Travers gazed at them in turn. 'Aunt tried to save him, but she was too late. She told me how it happened. You see, Uncle was a great hunter — big game and all that — '

'I had observed some results of his propensity in that direction,' the Doctor murmured.

'Aunt says he was dreaming he was in Africa again on a lion-hunt,' Travers continued. 'Suddenly a lion appeared and crouched to spring. Uncle fired but his rifle jammed, so he had to run for it.'

'I can just imagine it,' gulped Miss Frayle.

'Then Aunt saw him get out of bed, rush to the window, and she realised he was trying to escape from the lion in his dream. He walked through the open window on to the veranda. She screamed out to stop him: he awoke, but the shock caused him to stumbled against the railings, which gave way. He overbalanced and fell.'

'How ghastly!' Miss Frayle whispered.

Doctor Morelle tapped a cigarette on his thin, gold case.

'Your aunt doesn't yet know that he's dead?'

'No. I sent the manservant up to prepare her for the — for the worst before I rushed out to get the doctor.'

The Doctor applied the lighter to his Le Sphinx.

'Perhaps it would be as well if I saw her now,' he suggested.

'All right.' Travers turned to the midget wearily. 'Joseph, would you go upstairs and tell my aunt the Doctor would like to see her?'

'Very good, sir,' the midget replied gravely, and disappeared through the doorway.

Travers moved towards Doctor Morelle rather hesitantly. He smoothed the front of his jacket, and then drew his hands away quickly as he realised the blood-stains were there.

'There's something I ought to tell you,' he began evasively. 'It's about my aunt — '

'Yes?'

'Well — you'll find her rather a — well — curious woman.'

'Indeed?'

'She believes in astrology and clairvoyance — foretelling the future by dreams. That kind of thing.'

'I understand.'

'Before she married Uncle, she was very headstrong,' Travers went on. 'She toured with a circus, although she had no need to do so, and earned money by telling fortunes. Of course her family was horrified. It was at the circus that she met Joseph; her 'mascot' she called him, and when her family persuaded her to return home, she brought him back with her as a servant. This was twenty years ago. Joseph's been with us ever since. He's devoted to my aunt.'

Doctor Morelle drew at his cigarette contemplatively,

'There's one question I wish to ask you,' he began.

'Yes?'

'Was your dog at large at the time of the calamity?'

Travers paused for a moment. 'I think so — ' he said, then he nodded vigorously. 'Yes, he was — I remember now. We let him wander all over the house. You can't keep him in one room.'

Travers walked to the door, and held it open.

'Will you both come with me and wait in my aunt's room — her 'special room' she calls it — while I'll see if she'd like you to go upstairs? It's this way.'

They followed him.

Travers opened a door and clicked on the light. 'This is her room, I'll just go and tell her and then perhaps you'll come up?'

'At once,' said Doctor Morelle.

'Thank you.'

Miss Frayle followed the Doctor into the room and closed the door behind her.

She stared, fascinated by the peculiar decoration. Black curtains and drapes hung against a wall that might have been white, but which had a bluish tint reflected from the concealed blue panel lighting. The door was black with red panels edged with gold. On a blue table was a peculiarly shaped globe. It was twelve inches in diameter, composed of coloured strips of violet and orange, with red predominant. The globe revolved anti-clockwise from right to left.

'What is it?' Miss Frayle asked, fascinated by the device.

'A spectral lamp, used for hypnotic and mediumistic purposes,' Doctor Morelle replied. 'It would appear Mrs. Muir is a post-graduate student of the Great White Lodge of the Himalayas — a remnant of the Great University of Atlantis, which history tells us was sunk by the selfish powers of mankind about the year 254,666 BC. Some people believe that this great seat of learning knew metaphysical secrets that are ours for the seeking.'

It all seemed rather obscure to her. She gazed upwards.

'Just look at the ceiling! What does that star thing mean?'

'That, my dear Miss Frayle, is a magic pentacle, used, one would imagine by dabblers in the occult for the conjuration of devils.'

'Ooh!' Miss Fraye shuddered. She dragged her gaze from the pentacle. 'And there's a crystal here,' she noted. 'I wonder if Mrs. Muir really can see into the future?'

'I wonder?' There was a hint of scepticism in the Doctor's tone. He walked across to a bookcase. 'Quite an interesting assortment of literature,' he observed. He bent down to read the book titles: 'Astrology, and What the Stars Reveal'; 'Your Future in Your Hands'; 'The Ritual of the Black Mass'; and 'Adventures of Count Cagliostro'.'

'Whose he?'

'A notorious prestidigitator would, I

think, describe him.'

'A what?'

'A practitioner of legerdemain of the time of the French Revolution,' he amplified. He regarded her through narrowed eyes. 'Incidentally, Miss Frayle, has it not occurred to you that there is a suspicion of something deceptive concerning Colonel Muir's demise?'

Her eyes goggled behind their lenses.

'You mean he was murdered?' she gasped.

'Precisely, Miss Frayle.'

She turned to him, her eyes shining brightly. 'Don't tell me, Doctor. I know who did it!'

'Who?'

'That dog — probably aided and abetted by the midget,' she replied. 'Why, it's simplicity itself to anyone who uses scientific ratiocination and collates the facts as they present themselves — '

'Regrettably my words sound singularly banal when they are uttered by you, my dear Miss Frayle,' he reflected gloomily.

'I think you're very rude, Doctor,' she retorted with spirit.

'That is as may be,' he retorted indifferently. 'Nevertheless, perhaps you would gather your wits together sufficiently to enable you to slip out and telephone the police. Come! Come! Do not stand there as if you'd been hypnotised! Adjust your glasses and do as I say. Quickly, before the nephew returns.'

'Yes Doctor Morelle. The police . . . yes . . . ' she babbled confusedly, and made her way out of the room and down the stairs.

A few moments later Mr. Travers walked into the room. His frank, open face was tense with anxiety.

'I'm afraid my aunt cannot see you, Doctor. She is prostrate with grief — in bed — a terrible state.'

The Doctor clicked his tongue impatiently.

'Did you not tell her who I am?'

'Of course. I told her you were the great Doctor Morelle. She's heard of you, but — well, she says she prefers to see her own medical man.'

'No doubt she is apprehensive of my interrogating her?'

Travers frowned. 'Why should she be?'

Doctor Morelle calmly lit a Le Sphinx. He paused as he inhaled, then he said slowly:

'As you will soon learn when the police arrive, it was your aunt who caused Colonel Muir's death!'

'What!'

The other drew back, his lips twitching. 'No! No! I can't believe it!'

'You must bear the news with forti-tude,' the Doctor said. He reached for his stick. 'My task here is completed. It only remains for me to communicate my findings to Detective-Inspector Hood of Scotland Yard.'

* * *

Later the Doctor was warming his hands by the cheery fire in his study. He turned his back to the fire, and, clasping his hands behind him, faced Miss Frayle.

'I don't think it's fair, Doctor,' she was saying. 'You solved the crime without even meeting the murderess.'

'She refused to meet me.'

'That shouldn't have troubled you,' she pointed out. 'You had every right to *demand* to see her.'

'It was not necessary,' he replied, stifling a yawn. 'Mrs. Muir's guilt was obvious. In fact, it might be regarded as one of the simplest cases I have ever undertaken.'

'It's all very complicated to me. What gave you the clue?'

'The aunt's description to her nephew of how Colonel Muir fell from the window. This description was a complete fabrication. How could she have learned the details of his dream of being pursued by a lion if the shock of her awaking him caused his immediate fall and consequent instantaneous death? No one however gifted with clairvoyance or in occult arts, has yet been known to penetrate the mind of a sleeping person to that extent! She obliquely admitted her guilt when, on learning it was I who wished an interview, she refused to grant it. She had heard of my reputation as being the unrivalled — er — genius of scientific deduction, and feared my uncanny ability to pierce the veil of fabrication and ascertain the truth. She knew it would be futile to hide secrets from *me* — '

Miss Frayle was coughing, without any apparent need. He eyed her with a piercing glance.

'You are unimpressed, Miss Frayle?'

'No Doctor, go on with what you were saying.'

He continued to regard her suspiciously as he resumed,

'Detective-Inspector Hood subsequently advised me that the Aunt confessed to pushing the deceased to his doom while he was sleepwalking, with the object of benefiting earlier from his will.'

'Speaking for myself,' Miss Frayle hazarded, 'I would have thought that the bloodstains on Mr. Travers's coat would have been suspicious.'

'Since he carried the body in from the street, it was logical he would be covered with bloodstains.'

'I hadn't thought of that,' she said, 'but I tell you what I had thought might be a clue — '

He turned a withering glance upon her.

'Indeed? And since when, my dear Miss Frayle, have I evinced any interest in your vague theorising and obscure reasoning?'

She gaped at him, her mouth half open. She closed it, and made an attempt to shrug her shoulders with nonchalant indifference. He stubbed out his cigarette:

'When we write this case for my memoirs,' he murmured pensively, 'I believe an appropriate title would be 'The Curious Case of the French Marquis'.'

She found her voice to ask in studied astonishment:

'French Marquis? But — but the man was English.'

'Quite.'

'And he wasn't a marquis, either. He was a colonel.'

'Exactly.'

She stared at him. Really, what was he talking about?

'And anyway, it was the woman who really — '

'Precisely!'

'Then I — I don't understand.' She gave him a patronising smile, deciding to humour him. 'I mean, I don't see any connection between the title and — '

'I did not expect your somewhat pedestrian intelligence would grasp the resemblance between it and the mystery of Colonel Muir's demise,' he rasped. 'But I thought everyone knew the story of the old gentleman who, while attending church with his wife, fell asleep during the sermon. He dreamed he was a French aristocrat — a marquis during the time of the Revolution, and was about to be guillotined. As the knife fell his wife, observing him to be asleep, tapped him on the neck with her fan, and the shock killed him.'

'Poor man,' she murmured sympathetically. 'What a dreadful thing — and how awful for the wife too. Go on.'

'You still perceive no parallel between that story and the case of Colonel Muir?'

'No, I don't,' she replied with an infuriatingly puzzled little smile. 'He dreamed he was being chased by a lion.'

Doctor Morelle's face was a study in exasperation. Obviously exerting great control upon his feelings, he said through his teeth:

'Miss Frayle, I wonder would you be good enough to open the window? No — I do not propose to push you out — the drop would be insufficient! It is merely that I feel the need of a little air . . .'

THE END

DR. MORELLE MEETS MURDER
A CASE FOR DR. MORELLE
DR. MORELLE'S CASEBOOK
DR. MORELLE INVESTIGATES

We do hope that you have enjoyed reading this large print book.

Did you know that all of our titles are available for purchase?

We publish a wide range of high quality large print books including:
Romances, Mysteries, Classics
General Fiction
Non Fiction and Westerns

Special interest titles available in large print are:
The Little Oxford Dictionary
Music Book, Song Book
Hymn Book, Service Book

Also available from us courtesy of Oxford University Press:
Young Readers' Dictionary
(large print edition)
Young Readers' Thesaurus
(large print edition)

For further information or a free brochure, please contact us at:
Ulverscroft Large Print Books Ltd.,
The Green, Bradgate Road, Anstey,
Leicester, LE7 7FU, England.
Tel: (00 44) **0116 236 4325**
Fax: (00 44) **0116 234 0205**

Other titles in the
Linford Mystery Library:

THE LAS VEGAS AFFAIR

Norman Lazenby

Johnny Lebaron arrives in Las Vegas, leaving behind an unhappy marriage in New York. His hopes of a quiet vacation are dashed when he meets the beautiful Dulie Grande. Only recently out of jail, she seeks vengeance on the man who put her there — crooked casino owner Nat Franz. Johnny and Dulie, caught up in her vendetta against Franz, must fight for their lives against organised crime and a psychotic hit man with orders to kill them . . .